EARTH SIEGE

REALITY BLEED BOOK 8

J.Z. FOSTER

WINTER GATE PUBLISHING

To my daughter, Eleesha.

*I once heard her asking her mom, "How do I write **I don't love you anymore?"***

It was because I made her wait inside while I took out the trash.

Good thing she's cute.

PROLOGUE

As a conscript from Uzbek, Sarvar both barely understood the Russian language, and was given the poorest equipment.

"Here," the quartermaster had said as he dropped a dusty plastic container in front of Sarvar some weeks ago. He'd said something else too, but Sarvar hadn't understood a word of it. Eventually the man just pointed at the box then pointed at Sarvar's chest.

"Put. On."

It was CAG, defunct and several generations old, which Sarvar could tell that much at a glance. It even had the pronounced exposed battery on the back that had a habit of blowing up if hit too hard. Worse yet, the battery was visibly corroding.

Of course Sarvar wanted to ask why he had to wear it. Wouldn't it be better to *not* wear a CAG than to wear one with a corroded battery? If one of the mechanisms froze up, he would suddenly be locked in an armored tomb. What good would he be then? Or what if the air connection busted and he choked to death before he could get the helmet off?

But the Russian language wasn't his strong suit, and he didn't know how to complain.

He could only obey.

The thought crossed his mind, not for the first time, that he really should have paid more attention in school. He'd been thinking about it often since the Soviet Union collapsed, because he had a very thin understanding of what the hell was going on.

As a poorly trained conscript with terrible language skills, he was given a posting at a munitions factory, or maybe it was a chemical factory—he really wasn't sure. Mostly his job consisted of guard duty and watching cameras. At least it had until the quartermaster dropped off the ancient CAG.

And though Sarvar had poor language skills, he could see as well as anyone. He'd seen the videos of the monsters pouring out of Moscow.

Of course, those videos had come some time *after* Moscow had collapsed, when there was no longer a strong enough central authority to prevent such things from getting out.

So now, in full, vivid color, Sarvar got to watch monsters eat his fellow citizens on footage recorded by God-knows-who.

The same people who wouldn't attempt a conversation with him in broken Russian always seemed extremely interested in showing him videos of people getting eaten.

A man had waved him over to a screen. *"Sarvar!"*

Of course, Sarvar had tried to ignore him. He'd seen a man have his intestines pulled out through his ass yesterday. Why would he want to watch that again?

The man insisted. *"Sarvar!"*

There was really no way to ignore him at that point. Sarvar trotted over like a whipped dog while the man pointed at a video screen.

It was of the monster pulling someone's intestines out through his ass.

He'd already seen this one.

Sarvar looked at the man, who stared back with sympathetic eyes, like somehow watching this made it all better.

And he was left to wonder how long it would take the monsters to get to him.

How long until they were pulling *his* intestines out of his ass?

"They won't get here, the government is strong. They will stop the threat.

It won't spread." This was from the only other man on base who could speak Uzbek.

That man was dead now.

He died when the waves of monsters came pouring into their base.

Sarvar remembered the creatures. Most of them infected humans, but some were alien things without eyes. Large jaws and strings of spit dripped between their teeth. No two were alike.

He remembered one that had strange divots all over its body. Like something had just scooped out muscle and put skin all over it.

It didn't seem to be in any pain. At least, Sarvar imagined so as he watched it eating someone on a vid screen.

And the creatures were both strong and some even elegant in their assault.

Sarvar saw one snatch up his commanding officer into the air as it hung upside down from the ceiling, like some cartoon gorilla with gravity-defying strength. It snapped its jaws on the man's body as he screamed.

Sarvar ran under them, and it wasn't concerned.

Perhaps it was planning to eat him later? A midnight snack?

Waves of monsters swarmed over their base and killed most of the people there. It seemed that one bite could turn a person into something other than a human.

A once-man.

It had happened to the quartermaster. A creature bit him and shredded his arm off. As it ate the arm, the quartermaster writhed on the ground, not because he was dying, but because he was changing.

When he stood again, his eyes rolled into his head and his mouth stretched open in an eternal howl. Tentacles burst from his skin, and even with as little schooling as Sarvar had, he knew. . .

That's impossible. . .

How could they have grown so fast? How could they have changed him so quickly?

None of it made sense.

Now, with the creatures flooding through the facility, the soldiers had to lock off sections of the subterranean base. This occasionally meant the pathways between buildings were blocked off and filled with creatures. The only way to travel between portions of the base was to go up to land level and make a mad dash between the buildings.

Sarvar was thinking about one of those mad dashes right now as he touched the window sill of a glass door portal and stuck his head over the edge. It was hard to see because the inside of his CAG helmet kept fogging.

"*Dammit.*" He rubbed the outside of the helmet, which really didn't help much but he kept doing it anyway. He had to wait patiently and take shallow sips of air for the glass to clear.

He glanced back the way he'd come, but there was nothing in the hallway. It didn't look like there was anything outside either.

It didn't matter if he could see it. He *knew* there was something outside, but he was hungry.

Even now, his stomach growled.

"*Get the food and come back,*" his squad leader had told him.

Sarvar looked again.

Nothing.

He released a breath, and his glass fogged. With a groan, he leaned down and took small sips of air again to let the mask clear.

With the fog gone, he closed his eyes and tried to keep everything together. He tapped the open button, an old auxiliary switch that had to be pressed hard.

The button sank in and took a second before it clicked. The door gave a loud *clunk* and slowly ground into the wall. The internal gears screeched like dying birds as they cranked open. Sarvar winced.

He was sure something would hear it.

But nothing jumped out to grab him.

He peeked out the door but still didn't see anything.

Maybe he really was alone?

He took one step out, the nose of his rifle leading his way.

Nothing.

Another step onto the dirt between the buildings, and he was sure he was alone.

He still didn't ease up. He took a few cautious, exposed steps to the adjacent door, lined his badge with the scanner, and pressed the door open command.

A red light flared and scanned the badge.

There was a soft click.

But the door didn't budge.

He glanced to either side. Tall walls lined this narrow strip between buildings, but there was nothing else.

He leaned in and scanned his badge again.

Another soft click.

Didn't that mean it was unlocked?

It didn't move.

"Dammit." He rubbed his thumb over his badge and the scanner lens. He wasn't sure if it was rejecting his scan or if there was an error.

He scanned again.

The light blinked green. The door slid open with the sound of screeching metal. Apparently whoever's job it was to oil the doors was dead.

Then there was another sound of metal grinding. The door Sarvar had come through was closing.

"No!" He jolted forward and hit the open button, but it continued closing.

The door halfway closed, he thrust his arm into the shrinking gap, trying to hold it open. The door kept pushing. He groaned. It pressed onto his arm and pinched him in place, where it finally stopped.

Had he decent CAG and not this horrid antique, then he certainly would have been able to hold the door, but no, this CAG didn't cut it.

And he was stuck.

With sudden panic, he tried to jerk away, but the CAG armor was bulky.

"Oh shit. . ." he moaned. He tried to get his foot inside the gap for leverage.

It didn't budge.

He set his rifle down and got his other foot into the cranny of the door. He pushed in pained hope of pulling his arm free.

Grinding his teeth, he put all his strength into pulling. . .

And out of the corner of his eye, something stumbled into the path between buildings.

"Fuck!"

He didn't look again. He only yanked harder.

Thunk.

His arm came out. He stumbled backward and smacked his head against the wall.

That did it.

The armor was old. That one good blow to the back of the head was all it needed.

The armor's spinal support and one leg froze up completely. His momentum sent him sprawling onto his back.

His pulse pounding in his ears, Sarvar rolled around like an upside down turtle trying to find his feet. He teetered back and forth, one leg frantically kicking in the air as his hands flailed about. If only he could find something to grab.

With all the panicked breathing, his screen fogged to the point where he couldn't see anything clearly.

But then a blurry image smashed into view.

Sarvar couldn't help it. He screamed. "Help!" Of course, it was in his native language, not Russian. But why would that matter when no one could hear anyway? It really was just to make him feel better.

"Help me!" he roared. The blurred image savaged him. It smacked and clawed at his armor but hadn't gotten through.

"Someone help me!"

Another jumped on him and grabbed his leg. Sliding against the ground, he punched at the closest creatures.

Tentacles growing out of the thing's arms wrapped around his waist.

"Get off me!" He kicked with his good leg, but nothing seemed to bother the creatures.

One fit its mangled fingers into the grooves of his armor pieces and pulled so hard the bones snapped. The creature fell back, but another took its place.

Though Sarvar couldn't see for shit, he could hear them screeching and cheering. Maybe they were half starved because all the easy pickings were dead, and now they had to wait for the occasional fool to expose himself.

Oh yes, Sarvar was the life of the party now. He'd spent months with just a handful of conversations, and now *everything* wanted him.

All at once he was being dragged. Others piled onto him or slid their hands across his armor, trying to tear a piece off him.

Apparently, the shitty armor could hold off death for at least a little while, but that was the best it could do—delay the inevitable.

Sarvar had seen it happen.

It would just take time.

"Help me!" His armor scraped the ground. Where were they dragging him?

The power source on his back dragged across the ground, giving off the sound of a tin can being smashed under a boot. His body and the weight of the creatures damaged it further. The power went out in his right arm. It seized into place and stuck up in an awkward angle.

He continued to scream. *"Help me!"*

A woman with a bloody face pushed through the crowd and climbed on top of him. A thick, wigging stem jolted from between her teeth. She threw her head down. The stem cracked against his mask.

The woman's eyes rolled into her head, and the stem slithered across his glass lens, leaving streaks. Small hairs on the stem fit into the glass and moved back and forth to make the cracks larger.

Sarvar closed his eyes and sobbed.

This was how he would die. Frozen into place as the creatures slowly worked their way inside to tear him apart.

He remembered joking with his friends back in school.

"I want to die with a woman on top of me."

He'd then nod his head, hold out his hands, and thrust a few times to make his friends laugh.

It wasn't nearly as funny now.

The woman bucked on top of him. Her hands clawed into the

grooves of his armor so she could press her face down harder onto the glass.

He only hoped when that nasty, wrinkled stem pierced through the glass that it'd also go through his brain.

That's what Sarvar's life had amounted to in the end.

Hoping a hairy monster stem shoved into his face hard enough to kill him quickly.

The woman's head snapped in some other direction, like a dog when the doorbell rings.

It was so startling that Sarvar stopped sobbing and stared. The tentacles and hands that had been holding him let go. A new frenzy began.

Sarvar had no idea what was happening. He only felt their legs kick or smack against him as the creatures moved around in a bloody melee.

Something heavy shifted past him. Its movement kicked him hard enough to flip him onto his side. His right arm twisted painfully beneath him and might have been pulled out of socket. Grinding his teeth, Sarvar fit the fingers of his one good hand into the dirt and dragged his body across the ground. He wasn't heading in any particular direction. He only knew he didn't want to be in the middle of the melee.

The creatures kicked and stomped over him as he pulled away from the crowd. When he reached the edge, he clung to a wall and turned to look back.

The fog of his helmet still hindered his view, but the cracks let some air in, allowing the fog to ease up. He squinted. Apparently, the creatures had turned against one another and shredded each other's bodies in a furious assault.

One large-bellied man had a malformed arm with swollen, tentacle-like fingers. He had those fingers wrapped onto a person's neck as he tried to twist the other man's head off.

A woman frantically dug her hands into a diseased man's chest until she clawed something out and smashed it in her hand.

The woman with the stem in her mouth was mounting some other poor bastard, this one an evil creature like herself, and without the good fortune of a CAG helmet. She smashed her head down into his face and pulped it out the back, spraying the ground like a dumped can of spaghetti sauce.

Sarvar only watched in total confusion and amazement. He had no strength for anything else.

A fire bloomed on the other side. Then Sarvar saw what was happening. A squad of Soviet soldiers was making its way through the crowd of creatures, and flame troopers sprayed the warring creatures.

The crowd was being led by a woman in distinctly American CAG.

Sarvar's mouth opened wide in amazement.

His English was even worse than his Russian, but there wasn't a boy in all of the Soviet Union who didn't know all the best curse words used by the West.

Fuck. Shit.

Bitch.

And though her armor was only speckled red with blood, Sarvar had heard the rumors. He knew who she was.

And with both awe and gratitude, he whispered her name.

"The Red Bitch of Berlin."

1

ALICE HAD MANY NAMES.

Soldiers whispered them as she passed by.

The Red Bitch of Berlin, or sometimes simply *The Berlin Bitch.*

She'd garnered a reputation akin to Achilles or some ancient hero able to change the tides of battle with their abilities alone.

She'd walked through the streets of Berlin, her armor clean and gleaming in the sun.

The people would come out to see her. A silence would fall upon them, an honor of the lifetime to lay eyes upon her. They would whisper to one another.

"The Red Bitch of Berlin."

And Alice felt strong, with the gears of her CAG buzzing as she strode inside the city.

"We'll build you a team," Garin, the Grand Marshal of the Soviet forces, had said with the aid of a translator. His voice was gruff and growling with his replacement chin. *"I'll gather the best killers in the Soviet Union. All with capable English. I'll put them under your command. We'll designate a dropship crew for your missions.*

We'll turn back the monsters.

We'll win this war."

She conducted twelve drops within two weeks' time of her new directive. Though she was but one person, she was an army unto herself.

With every drop, they rolled back the enemy's advances.

Against Alice, the once-men went insane and killed themselves, while she disrupted the eyeless cronux horrors' connection to the hive mind. They would lose coordination, which made easy kills for the Soviet marksman.

But they had only fought small groups, not the horde again.

She was now a *Ghost*, a rank and designation that fell outside of the branches of the military.

She could coordinate her own missions and negotiate her own purposes with Soviet command.

The only person she was to take orders from was Roles himself, and his last transmission was clear. *"We're drawing back Moller for the time being. But you'll stay with the Soviets. I'll build our defense while you contain the threat. You're the only one who can."*

Roles sent a half dozen members of an American support team into Berlin to see to the treatment of her armor and coordination of her missions and well being.

When she came back each night, the team would swarm her, tools in hand, and take apart her armor to meticulously inspect and repair before she went back out again the next day.

A personal physician saw to a regiment of stims, protein, and vitamin injections to keep her in top shape.

And she felt it.

She'd been confused before. Her thoughts had been thick like mud, which made it hard to think.

But not now.

It was like someone had opened the hood and put a little more oil in her engine.

She was good. Smooth. Perceptive.

Focused.

And now, bright and early, she was on a new mission with the sun barely peeking over the horizon. A dropship had dispatched

Alice and her team into the thick of battle at a factory not far from Berlin.

Garin had picked it personally.

"There are weapons and fuel cells essential for the war effort there," he'd told her.

That didn't matter to her. She didn't need to know why Garin wanted her there.

She was there to kill them.

When the ship let them loose and her drop cage slammed into the dirt, Alice's pulse pounded in her ears.

The Soviet team in their glaring red armor came out of their cages, snapped rifles up, and fired rounds nearly instantly.

They were dangerous people.

So was she.

A horde of once-men roared at them, the impact of the cages drawing attention. A mass of claws and teeth hungry for flesh.

But Alice wasn't afraid. A hyper awareness settled on her. She could feel her heart in her chest. . .

Thump-thump.

. . .along with the loud exhale as she let go of the breath she'd held.

The world moved slowly for her as the Soviets' rifles flashed in her peripheral vision. As they formed a line, the Soviets yelled to each other in accented English.

A horror was coming for them. One that had been eating away at their empire.

But the soldiers weren't afraid.

This wasn't their first time.

They knew what she could do.

Less than a dozen feet from the mob, Alice stepped forward, her foot pounding the ground as if to make it quake. She raised her fist into the air.

A ripple of insanity flowed through the horde as their diseased and corrupted minds broke.

She was more than a person now.

She was a ghost.

She didn't need to find and take hold of the whole horde. Alice saved her strength and broke the minds of the first wave.

The once-men frenzied and tore at those near them while the Soviet soldiers moved forward, rifles firing.

Bullets smashed into soft flesh before Alice's eyes, and shell casings clattered near her feet. She took another step forward, and though she did not make the world shake, her presence was heavy within the hive mind. Inside the dark void of that world, Alice moved with the force of an earthquake. Her presence shook that world and broke the red veins that connected the cronux.

In the real world, the monsters either fell to their knees and screamed with madness or turned upon one another. As one died, Alice's mind moved to another and shattered its will.

An infected woman collapsed to the ground and howled. Red tears poured from her face, and the other once-men tore her apart. A man with an elongated neck turned to batter those closest to him.

A woman with a stem from her mouth ran toward a wall and smashed her head against it until she was only beating a stump. A soldier sprayed fire onto her.

Alice could feel the parasites within the woman shriek inside the hive mind as they popped from the heat.

More fought and more died.

Alice stomped forward, one fist raised to focus her control. Alongside her, a Soviet flame soldier let loose a kiss from his torch, burning the once-men even as they struggled against each other.

Alice shifted her hand in the air. The mob parted. Their screams were so loud it was nearly deafening. Alice turned off her CAG's exterior sound, which made the world go silent inside her helmet except for the voices of her team.

One Soviet soldier fired into the chest of a once-man, pulping it until it could no longer stand. It fell back, and others dove onto it. Another soldier kicked his boot into a creature and hurled it into a crowd of reaching hands.

All around them, the creatures' flesh bubbled and ruptured from the searing flames. Alice's team moved past them, and as the parasitic monsters died, the cronux came.

A four-legged creature with the thickness of a rhinoceros stomped into view. It had a mouth the size of a truck, its lips pulled back with a wet sneer.

The Soviets didn't wait for Alice's command. They each fired rounds, peppering the beast's hide as it charged them.

More cronux scaled the walls of the building. Alice could feel them within the hollows of the hive mind.

She had a reputation amongst the men—*The Berlin Bitch*—but the cronux knew of her too.

Alice's reach spread like a reaching fog within the hive mind, and though the cronux did not taste fear like humans did, they were not mindless beasts.

If the Archon was a god, then she too was divine.

But they still came.

With clawed fingers and snapping teeth, they hurled their bodies at Alice.

But she was not the only threat amongst them.

Garin had promised her a team of hardened killers, and he had delivered.

The Soviets dashed forward and took cover behind buildings and destroyed vehicles. They fired their rifles and picked their targets while Alice spread horror and madness amongst them, enough to dull the sharp edges of the cronux mind.

The rhino-sized beast charged forward while a Soviet soldier took a knee and aimed his shoulder-mounted launcher. A missile surged out and hit the beast in the mouth, exploding between its jaws.

The creature thrashed about, flaps of its destroyed jaw waving in the air.

A group of three other soldiers focused their fire on a leaping cronux. They peppered it with enough rounds that it was dead before it hit the ground.

The team moved forward, each with a job and part to play as they had done before.

Waves of the creatures came at them. As Alice's team cut them down, one began to run.

Alice focused her mind like a blade and shoved it into the creature's head.

It fell from the building it was clinging to, and the Soviet soldiers hurried to it, rifles firing. It jittered with each shot until it went still.

Birds came at them. Alice waved her hand.

Simple, dumb things, they only careened into the wall and plastered it with their broken bodies. The flame soldier stepped closer and sent a blast at the quivering pile, inciting a shriek from one hundred voices.

When all was done, Alice heard a voice on the command.

"What about this one?" The soldier's voice buzzed over her comms with accented English.

Alice turned to see a man in old CAG hunched against the wall.

"He's fine. I don't feel anything inside him." She turned the exterior microphone back on and approached the man.

He only pointed up at her and spoke with a trembling voice.

"The Red Bitch of Berlin."

After Alice's team swept through the base and mopped up the remaining creatures, they were picked up and returned to Berlin as Garin's regular forces moved in to secure the area.

The liberated medical supplies, munitions, and soldiers would soon make their way back, but the Soviets couldn't continue resupplying Berlin like this. They had to move forward.

As Alice came back onto the base, the team hurried her into a hangar bay where they'd set up.

They went through a series of questions, asking her if she was hurt, what she'd seen, and what she felt.

A psychological team would review her answers, while a medical team attended to her wounds. Lastly, a tactical team would implement the details she'd gathered from the cronux.

She stepped onto a platform. The team came onto her with cordless drills to disassemble her armor.

They worked with the speed of a pit crew in a car race, removing plates one at a time to be repaired and cleaned and taking Alice down to the black skin suit with the circulatory mesh she wore beneath the CAG.

Then a woman brought her a military uniform. She slipped it over the skin suit. All markings of designation and rank had been removed from the simple Orbital Corps officer's uniform, all except one round, black patch with a silver center on her sleeve.

Ghost.

Garin had a plan. He wanted to move deeply into the heart of Poland.

"We're going to retake Warsaw. There is a civilian population under siege and capable airfields to conduct aerial operations." He'd told her that before he called her in to speak to his officers.

She headed that way. Some of the officers were newly appointed after most of the leadership was killed during a failed coup.

She expected they all might hate her. The Americans and the Soviets had been in a Cold War for longer than most of them had been alive, but when the door to the command room opened, the entire room fell silent.

And though no one said it, Alice knew they were all thinking it.

The Red Bitch of Berlin.

The meeting went on as Garin discussed his plan to move forward, but it was all in Russian. A member of her coordination team accompanied her and translated things when she asked him too, but Alice didn't find it necessary. It was only when Garin gestured toward her that she focused once more.

"Will you explain their structures?" Garin asked in accented English.

Alice straightened from her spot near the wall, and all eyes turned on her. A tangle of blonde hair hung in front of her face, a stark contrast to the Soviet women who had their heads shaved or their hair pulled tightly back.

Alice cleared her throat. When she spoke, it was hoarse. She didn't speak much these days.

She went through details of the cronux and the parasites. Even the elites that seemed to be more powerful than the others.

"There was one on Felicity. It could steal the faces of its victims." A shiver ran through her. "Someone named the damn thing Scalpie. He was unique, but there are others that evolve and change and are more powerful than the rest. You've all seen the Worm."

The Soviets all had a basic understanding of English but some did pause to ask questions or speak with translators. When the once-men came up, she explained the only methods to cure them.

"I only know of two ways. Inject the parasite with cryo. Some other type of poison might work, but I don't know anything for certain. It's only been done once."

"And the other way?" an officer asked.

Alice made a cutting gesture at her arm. "Take the whole limb off."

They went through the abilities of the once-men and who coordinated them, but the room fell deathly silent when Alice spoke of the Harbingers.

She took a deep breath before speaking. "They're powerful beings with mental control over squads of cronux. The Harbingers themselves evolve at a quick pace. The one I saw on Felicity was learning how to speak when we killed him."

Garin cleared his throat. He'd heard all of this before, but he wanted them to hear it from her. "Tell them about the Archon."

An itch crawled up Alice's back, as if the room suddenly chilled.

"The Archon," she began, her voice barely a croak. "They see him like a god."

An officer with old, gray eyes rubbed the bristles on his chin. He spoke in Russian to a young translator standing at attention.

"There has been a video of the Archon," the translator said. "Is he simply like them, only more powerful?"

How could they understand? None of them were inside the hive mind.

None of them felt the weight of the Archon's soul.

She leaned forward, and the tangle of hair dangled in front of her eyes. She tried to resist it, but a smile slid across her face.

"He's a baby," she whispered, if only to keep herself from laughing, though there wasn't anything joyful about it. "A baby god finding his place in the world. He's more than strong. He's changing." She shook her head. "I don't know what he can do yet."

After Alice answered their questions as best she could. She left them with one final thought.

"We need to find the gates and destroy them. The one near Moscow is finished. No more of them can come into the world. If we do that, we can win the war."

When she was finished, she headed back to the room on the base the Soviets had given her. It might have been bugged. It likely was.

She didn't care.

She liked to be alone.

But just last night, as she'd laid in bed staring up at the ceiling, she had a realization.

She didn't have to sleep anymore.

She came out of the bed and sat on the cold floor to stare at the wall.

The cold didn't bother her either.

Few things did anymore.

But now, as she entered the room and the door locked behind her, she stripped her clothes off and sat on the cold floor once more.

She stared at the wall.

Her brain felt as though it were crawling inside her head. A soft, gentle movement, as though shifting its weight around.

Rearranging things.

Was it four days? Was it five? How many had she gone without sleep?

She only pretended like she still needed it.

All just for show.

No. Not for show. For Eli.

There it was. But why then hadn't she called him? She had time these last few days.

She had time now. . .

After a breath, she decided she would later.

Her mind just wasn't there. How could she call him when all she saw was red when she closed her eyes?

What would she even say to him?

God, she was exhausted, but only mentally.

Her body tired just like anyone else's, but it was no worse than the feeling after a long jog. She had stims to help focus, but even they weren't truly necessary.

But what was necessary anymore?

Sitting on the floor, she focused on her breathing. Taking the air in and out, she wondered . . .

Did she still have to breathe?

Was she still human?

A moment passed before she took another breath.

She wasn't yet ready to find out.

2

IT MIGHT HAVE BEEN hard to get Marat out of the Soviet Union, but he wasn't aware.

He'd woken up in West Germany, apparently evacuated while unconscious. Lacey Moller had come with him, but Alice Winters had stayed behind.

At least that's what Moller told him. He hadn't had much time to think about it.

He hadn't had much time to think about *anything* after waking up from surgery.

At the moment, he sat in a cushioned chair and glared at a glass container. It was the most comfortable chair he'd sat on in his entire life, but he certainly wasn't relaxed.

"Hey, you wanna see something?" one of the younger doctors had said two hours ago. Marat hadn't even responded when the man pulled a glass container off a cart with what looked like two burnt steaks. Fat, ugly steaks. *"These were your lungs. Fun, right?"*

No. Not fun.

The doctor had been grinning like a fool when he set the container on a table next to Marat and left. Marat spent the first few minutes wondering what the hell he was supposed to do with them, then the rest of the time wondering if the doctor was fucking with him.

In his short time in the irradiated wasteland of East Germany, Marat's lungs had started to melt inside his chest, causing him to drown on the peeling tissue lining.

It hadn't been a lovely experience.

Still, to blame the German radiation for the poor condition of his lungs would have been too kind to the fact that he'd been a smoker all his life.

"No more smoking," the head surgeon had told him when he woke up. *"You've got forty thousand dollars worth of equipment in your chest, and it has to be carefully calibrated. No more smoking."* He'd handed Marat a pack of nicotine gum.

Marat chewed the whole pack in an afternoon.

It tasted like shit.

But he wasn't concerned about that now. He was still looking at his rotted lungs and considering how they used to be a piece of him. An important piece, in fact.

He laid back in the chair and lifted his shirt to see the massive scar. That was new too, obviously, but it wasn't the worst thing about the whole experience.

He could *feel* his new lungs in his chest. It was an odd sensation to be fully aware of his lungs rising and falling while they pressed around the inside of his chest. It happened with each and every breath. It made him nervous.

And when he was nervous, he liked to smoke.

I need a cigarette.

He got out of his seat and moved to his things. He was still in a gown, but didn't mind. He hated how it flapped open in the back. There was something unsettling about the idea that any person who stepped into the room might catch a look at his bare ass.

The Germans had put him in a recovery room after the surgery, which he had to say, was much better than anything he'd seen in the Soviet Union, though it was an all-white, sterile place.

But it felt odd he couldn't see any cameras, especially after he was told there wouldn't be a guard outside his room. That had been a strange moment after waking up from surgery and talking to the doctor, then seeing everyone leave.

Marat had sat in the room in total silence for a few good minutes waiting for someone to enter. No one did.

So with no guard, he was *sure* they had a camera in here somewhere. Moller told him they wouldn't bug his room, but he couldn't believe it. The Soviet Union would shove a camera up someone's ass if they thought they'd get a good view, and he highly doubted the European Federation or the Americans were any different.

He took a glance around the room.

Someone was watching. He knew it.

As carefully as he could, he slid the beat-up pack of cigarettes out of his pants pocket as well as his electro lighter.

He stiffened and eyeballed the room as he went to the door.

He was allowed out of the room, but the pack of cigarettes along with feeling *every single breath* in his chest made him feel guilty.

"*O-pen,*" he said awkwardly. He wasn't sure it would.

The door slid into the wall.

Apparently, it spoke shitty English.

Marat stuck his head out.

A few orderlies and medical staff were milling about, but no one looked his way.

Holding the gown closed to hide his ass, Marat made his way to the restroom.

The hospital hallway was rounded and was painted the same sterile white as his room. Windows lined the walls, and Marat could see that it was raining. Marat shuddered. This close to the border, and the rain was still toxic like in East Germany. You could tell by the murky swirls of white in the sky.

He got inside the restroom and took a moment to look under each stall. Satisfied the room was empty, he got into one, locked it, and climbed onto the toilet.

He slid one cigarette out. He lit it with the electro lighter and took a puff.

Heavenly.

The cigarette scratched an itch.

He stretched toward the exhaust fan and exhaled.

Everything seemed to relax inside, and if only for that moment, life was good.

He took another puff and breathed deeply. He exhaled into the fan again.

Then the door opened.

"*Fuck,*" he mumbled. The cigarette dropped between his feet into the toilet. He flagged the smoke toward the fan and got down.

He was going to have to pretend like he was sitting on the can.

"—they nuked it," said one voice.

"Did they really? That close to Moscow?" a different man answered.

"You kidding? They actually *nuked* Moscow too."

"Serious business."

Marat had a faint idea what they were talking about, but he wasn't sure. The men moved over to the urinals.

"Won us the Cold War, didn't it?" the first man said. "Doesn't matter anymore, though. That's all the talk. The gate was in a bunker and they nuked it. It's smooth sailing from here."

Marat stayed in until he heard the people leave, then he slowly climbed out.

They thought it was over? That the bunker was nuked and it was all finished?

Marat worked at that place. Hell, he lived at that place.

It was built to withstand a nuke.

Moller had spent the last few days preparing for her new directive from Roles.

"I need you to secure some live parasites, and I don't want Alice Winters to know anything about it."

Roles had said it like the task wasn't impossible.

The parasites themselves were highly dangerous, and Alice could feel them with her mind.

Moller still couldn't understand the scope of Alice's powers, but she'd seen firsthand what the woman could do. Moller had detailed and recorded all of it in reports to Roles.

But now she was at a loss. How in the world was she going to get a parasite aboard a transport, let alone hide it from Alice?

Roles had only one thing to say about her concerns.

"You'll think of something."

Intel inside the Soviet Union was still nearly impossible to get. The Soviets had an automated aerial system that could shoot down American planes, along with a satellite defense dubbed *The Iron Curtain*, which emitted disruptive imaging signals to prevent American spy satellites from much imaging. Anything other than stealth-focused aircraft was going to get shot down.

The Soviets lost control over much of their systems when Moscow and Leningrad fell, but some systems were still active and running on autopilot.

They were in talks about getting reconnaissance from the European Federation and American planes, but even after all that happened, Garin was concerned about giving free access to the Americans.

"I've already survived one coup attempt. I might not survive another."

Politics were always a delicate thing to balance.

As best Moller could tell, Alice's father, U.S. President John Winters, was having his own problems. Congress was threatening him for not taking stronger actions against the Soviet Union after the assassinations, and there were growing conspiracies throughout the country that he was working with the Soviet Union. Civil conflict brewed in South America with the collapse of the peace accords, and the debt crisis in the European Federation had only worsened with news of the instability in the U.S.

Moller had read all of that the day before. She decided to stop before she got to the part about the insurgencies in the South.

None of that was Moller's problem for the time being. Her concern was making sure the cronux stayed contained. But the intel on the situation inside the Soviet Union was so poor, it was hard to make any real judgement calls.

With the Soviet's intelligence network in complete disarray, they were mostly blind to what was happening, but Moller had a pretty good idea.

Every major city was burning. Every train transport station was overrun.

People were dying.

The cronux were building an army, and any person more concerned with politics than the alien threat was a fool at best and dangerous at worst.

She ignored the politics now as she sat in a command room hunched over a datapad displaying the most current maps of the Soviet Union. Everyone knew the maps were incomplete. A cup of coffee was steaming next to her—her third of the day so far.

She had a digital pen in hand and made notes on the map next to the cities she had reliable information on.

Infested.

Besieged.

Destroyed.

She set the pen down on the table and rubbed her eyes.

How in the hell was she going to get in there and gather a parasite to *safely* bring out? How could she even—

"*Moller!*" One of the officers on the base strode toward her. "The commie wants to talk with you."

"Marat Ivanov?"

The man nodded. "He's outside losing his goddamn mind."

Marat couldn't help it. He had a cigarette plugged into his mouth and was puffing away. He was wise enough to head between the barrack buildings where the enlisted men smoked.

His hand was still jittering though. Why in the hell was it always jittering?

Moller stepped into view, and Marat had to pause.

He still wasn't used to seeing her out of CAG. Her curves were all the more clear, not to mention what a few days of rest and a shower could do to a woman.

"Marat." She came closer. "I'm glad to see you up and walking around, but you really shouldn't be—"

"They say gate is down," Marat interrupted, his English sputtering.

Moller nodded. "The Soviets launched a nuclear weapon at it. The nuke disabled the gate."

Marat shook his head and stepped closer to her. He leaned forward and pointed at the ground. "I live in that place for years. It's too strong. One missile will not destroy."

Moller frowned. "Marat, right before we left Berlin, I spoke with Alice. She can feel everything. She felt the gate go down. The whole place was destroyed. It must have been."

Marat stuck the cigarette into his mouth and took a long drag. He exhaled, blowing it all out, and then stabbed the end onto the brick wall. "No. I don't know what is happen, but I know that bunker is still there. The gate is still going."

Moller looked away from Marat, and he could tell she was considering things.

He wanted to move closer, to reach out and put his hand on her. He also wanted to get as far away from here as possible and never see another cronux in his life.

She met his eyes, and that was the first time he noticed her eyes were green.

"Then I'm going back. I have to check it."

Marat didn't even think before he spoke.

"I go too."

3

JOHN FELT LIKE A CORPSE. All they needed to do was bury him.

Some were even trying.

"I have some very serious questions about what is going on within the administration," Tom McIntyre, majority leader of the U.S. Senate, said to a nodding host on live TV. *"For God's sake, the Soviets assassinated half the executive branch of government, and now we're out there fighting for them? It gives one pause."*

Of course the host nodded and even went so far as to question why nuclear weapons hadn't been deployed immediately.

John leaned back and shook his head.

Why didn't I turn half the world into a sea of fire? Why didn't I decide to obliterate men, women, and children who had nothing to do with their government's actions? Why didn't I choose to become the greatest mass murderer on the face of the planet?

That was all John could take before turning away. Ben McAndrews, his chief-of-staff, had wanted him to watch it, but John refused.

"You watch and let me know if there's anything important. I've got work to do."

John did note that the bastard McIntyre, with the synthetic vein and lack of feeling in his face, had done his best to remember to blink while on camera, but John could still see that vein pumping into his head.

A crowd of protestors had formed in front of the White House and were growing by the day. They were all getting stirred up with fear and conspiracy theories. McIntyre's interview hadn't even been the worst. Some freshman firebrand Congressman had even gone so far as to *speculate* if John hadn't been in on everything.

"You just have to wonder why he's so willing to do their bidding."

Do their bidding? What a crock.

So far John hadn't agreed to much of anything beyond preventing the Soviet's extermination in Berlin. John had dispatched a diplomat to negotiate on aerial support to advance the Soviet forces, but that was hardly a sure thing.

Even with the world burning, politics were still a delicate thing.

"Imagine if one of our planes gets shot down by one of the Soviet's automated systems. They'll hang you," McAndrews had offered.

Likely, he wasn't wrong, but John was hardly concerned about that. He knew what those creatures could do, and if they could be contained in the Soviet Union at the cost of John's political career, so be it.

I wanted to retire anyway.

But the stress and the workload were wearing on him. It was too much burden for the skeletal crew his administration was running now.

In his office, he took calls with his ambassadors in the European Federation and the governors of each state.

"Are you expecting to push Congress into implementing the draft? Should we be preparing?" one governor asked.

God in Heaven, that's all the motivation the mob would need to break the gates down and tear him into pieces. A draft for their sons and daughters to go fight with the Soviet Union.

It wouldn't come to that.

He hoped not.

But the world was a diseased and broken place. The only certainty was that the next disaster was going to be worse than the last.

The news stories of the day had a common theme. They believed America to be a failing enterprise.

Prominent journalists and media personalities all had their own opinions as to why.

Too many wars.

A shrinking middle class.

Social unrest.

Riots.

Poverty.

Crime.

America was formed as a dream, strong and healthy.

Now it laid on a bed, chewed apart by its problems—a dying super power.

What had happened to the Land of the Free and the Brave?

An average personal debt of one hundred thousand dollars and a declining life expectancy, that's what happened.

Things were bad.

A second American Civil War was something that had gone from being discussed in academia to being debated over the dinner table.

Americans saw each other as their enemy, and members of opposing parties were vile and evil. It wasn't a matter of if the Civil War would come.

But when.

John had given a speech once. He diagnosed the ills of the American people and had taken to the Senate floor with his ideas.

It might have been a snoozer by most accounts, but he ended his speech with a line that carried on every news station that night.

"If you only like Democracy when your side wins, then you don't like Democracy."

His approval ratings were high then.

Funny how things can change.

As if on cue, McAndrews entered into his office. He headed to the window and peeked through the curtains. "We're going to have to do something about that."

The crowd was only getting bigger and the signs more extreme. They declared everything from calling John a communist and a Soviet sympathizer to outright demanding his imprisonment and execution. The people hurled slurs and curses while security staff patrolled the gate to keep the crowd from attacking.

There were a hundred or more here, along with protests in several major cities.

"What do you suggest? Offer them my head?" John said. He'd seen the size of a crowd.

McAndrews winced. "No, I'd prefer not to do that. They might want mine next."

"Funny."

McAndrews stepped away from the window, letting the curtain close. "Hey, I'm just glad *John Winters* doesn't make for a good rhyme. Just imagine if your name was Lester."

John waved his hand. "As always, good thoughts."

"That's what I'm here for. I have your daily schedule loaded on your datapad." McAndrews rounded to the front of John's desk and let out a sigh. "Did you end up watching the rest of that McIntyre interview?"

"Of course not." John shook his head. "I'm trying to work out a deal with the European Federation for flyovers in Soviet airspace. I don't have time for television."

"Unfortunately, Mr. President, when the majority leader of the Senate wants to get on TV and talk shit, I think it's noteworthy." He tapped the datapad.

John hissed. "Play the damn thing then."

McAndrews hit a button, and a video played. There was a side-by-side shot of McIntyre with the same television host as before.

The video began mid-interview.

"...of course I don't think the president is a bad person," McIntyre said, the vein pulsing on his forehead. *"He's just a fish out of water. The shoes are too big for him."*

The host, a very clean man with bright white teeth, stood in great contrast to McIntyre's sickly yellowed skin. He nodded with each word. *"But Majority Leader, there are a growing number of people everyday with questions as to why President Winters seems more interested with helping the Soviet Union than trying to push back at them for the assassinations. How can we possibly not be in a war with them after they did this?"*

"Good God, didn't they say all this already? Are they just repeating themselves now?" John asked.

McIntyre stared at the camera. It seemed to go on far too long before he realized he hadn't blinked in sometime.

Blink.

His paper-thin eyelids closed and opened so slowly it seemed like McIntyre had forgotten how halfway through.

"Well, I suppose not everyone has the backbone required by a president."

"So what is it that you're suggesting?" the host said. *"That John Winters is a coward?"*

John looked up at McAndrews. "Do I really need to watch this?"

His chief-of-staff nodded.

"I won't comment on that at this time, but I will tell you that I've been in discussions with the speaker of the House, and they are looking into forming articles of impeachment if the president isn't able to fully perform the duties of his job."

"Impeachment?" The host raised his eyebrows. John practically snorted. It was clear as day that the whole interview was staged. *"And what of the rumors of his daughter?"*

The hair stood on the back of John's neck.

"—that the president pulled strings to have her transitioned out of Libya after the fall of Tripoli while other Americans remained stationed?"

McIntyre stared at the camera with dry, veiny eyes. This time he didn't bother to blink. John felt like the man was staring directly at him.

"No comment," McIntyre croaked.

McAndrews paused the video.

"When the hell did this air?" John asked.

"Couple of hours ago."

"And you're just now telling me?"

McAndrews lifted his shoulders. "You said you didn't want to be involved, but I figured right now you didn't have a choice."

John felt the urge to throw something but kept his composure. "Where in the hell did that idiot even find out about Libya? This is the first I've heard it out in the public."

McAndrews shook his head. "Me too. So we have to go into damage control then."

"Damage control for *what?* My reputation? It's in tatters as is. If all these people are intent on tearing me apart, then they can do it after we've contained the end of the world."

John suddenly thought of the Book of Secrets and all the passages from past presidents writing about their decisions.

Would he even have time to write a passage himself?

John took a deep breath and exhaled. He'd spent so much time on his heels. It was time to get back to his old self.

"This administration is going to prioritize the cronux threat. We're going to recruit staff members that can get on board to help make sure we don't crash the damn economy while we're trying to save the world."

"Here's the thing. The midterms are coming up and—"

"Ben." John rested his hands on his desk and leaned closer. "If you bring up the midterms again, I'm going to fire you. Now whatever your schedule is, clear it, and get me a list of names to fill our positions."

McAndrews snorted with some irritation. "Right-o then."

Roles was both a liar and a killer—an expert at both, in fact. But his real skills came with seeing the *big picture* along with the *little details* others missed.

"*Hmmm.*"

Sometimes, all he needed was a quiet spot and a drink in hand to help the gears turn.

He tapped his fingers on the desk as he brought a drink to his lips. Roles himself designed the designation of *Ghost* for Alice Winters. It put her outside the military chain of command.

And directly beneath him.

The designation gave her free rein to conduct her mission, and Roles didn't feel the need to micromanage her.

The best way to use an attack dog was to let it off the leash.

Alice Winters might be all that was standing between those monsters and the end of the world.

But Alice was a hammer, and, based on Moller's reports, possibly insane.

She wasn't a thinker.

Roles was.

"Hmmm."

He took another sip.

He was still getting reports, though not as effectively without Moller in Berlin. It didn't matter. She was his top operative, and he needed her elsewhere.

The new reports told of a series of victories, where Alice Winters and her new team of Soviet commandos were dropping in and *rolling* back the influence of the Janissary, the cronux commander.

Janissary.

That gave him a soft chuckle.

Where the hell did Alice get these names?

Roles took another drink and exhaled deeply as condensation rolled down his glass.

Being a *big picture* guy, he couldn't help but think the Janissary was giving in a little *too* easy. Sucking Alice Winters and her commandos a little farther out with each new drop.

The Janissary was a bastard and a smart one. Roles knew it in his gut. The Janissary was planning something.

But what?

That wasn't the only concern.

Apparently, the Archon had fallen off the radar.

A mass of monsters were *gone* because the country was in such chaos they couldn't even figure out where the damn things were. Even Alice couldn't feel them.

At least that was what she'd told Roles.

He took another sip. *"Hmmm."*

But the Archon. . . Roles had seen videos of him. There was nothing particularly intelligent about how he fought. All in all, he seemed to be just a stronger, faster beast than the rest of them.

Then again, Alice had said he was a god and he was young.

So Roles had to wonder. . .

Maybe the Archon was just a baby learning how to walk.

So what would happen when he found out how to use his legs?

Roles finished the glass. "Hmmm."

4

A MASSIVE, green chemical fire clawed into the red evening sky.

The horde had assaulted a chemical facility, and at some point, a massive fire erupted inside the compound. The flames turned green as things sizzled inside. The smell of cooked meat floated in the air.

They fed the flames with whatever they found. The heat was so intense that the skin on some of the cronux charred black as they threw chemicals upon the flames.

It wasn't just the man-made chemicals; it was the cronux with their bellies full of acid.

The great, wandering beasts had a dull understanding of things, but powerful brains to estimate trajectory as they launched themselves into the air.

A natural call of devotion flowed into some. They entered the compound and erupted. Their unnatural wastes set the whole place ablaze even against the man-built safety precautions inside the facility.

Others craved this religious rite and threw themselves into death. One sauntering and ambitious beast with no natural chemicals held a metal barrel in his hands. His skin shriveled and popped as he walked toward the flames.

The pain reverberated through the horde, and they returned it with praise. He proved himself worthy as the fire overtook him and heated the barrel.

Whatever was in the contents of the barrel exploded and sent a surge of blue flames into the air.

The cronux howled in ecstasy and worship.

Inspired by the devotion, another cronux wobbled up on powerful legs carrying a large barrel of chemical waste.

He heaped himself into the flame and burst, though he hadn't gone deep enough. The acid inside the barrel sprayed his brothers who were some distance away. They shrieked as the acid ate away their bodies.

Damaged, their bodies were spent, and their brothers gave them no time to consider sacrifice.

Some resisted and fought as the others grabbed them and hurled them into the flames. Others accepted their fate and ran toward the fire to see an honorable destruction.

All screamed in pain and thrashed as the fires consumed them, and a religious fervor overtook their brothers.

They were wild beasts. Most anything could provoke their lust for blood. They turned on each other with claws and teeth. The weak and the wounded were hurled inside, while the strong continued to kill.

This was all in praise of the Archon, who hunched near the fire and looked into the dancing flames.

Even as they tore and ravaged each other, none dared come close to the Archon, for he was deep in thought.

He was trying to remember how he got there.

He knew that some days ago he stepped onto a train. It had been a clean metal structure before, but now it was coated with blood. A cronux had grown to the length of the cars. The creature looked little more than a melted pile of flesh with screaming faces, but the Archon knew it had purpose.

Its body had thin wisps that reached into the walls and paneling of the train. Energy flowed through it.

It was in pain. That much had been obvious by the howling of the creature.

But though it suffered, it never ceased its duty.

Its life was one of service, and it submitted to its greater purpose.

So too did the Archon.

But his purpose and his suffering was much greater than the creature within the train.

He was a god, and his brain was altered.

He was changing.

Pockets of air sizzled and popped within the soft tissues of his brain, leaving voids that filled with acidic fluids.

He struggled to think with his brain continually adjusting, but the movement also enlightened him and somehow activated a part of him that was never meant to exist.

Beauty.

There was beauty in the suffering of the cronux within the train, and there was art in the land the Archon had seen through the window as the train sped past.

But he could make it more.

So much more.

He would change it. He would remake the world.

But first, he would have to remake himself.

Ahh, there it was.

He remembered now.

He stood up, and the cronux around him howled their praise and fell to the ground in submission. Whatever quibbles they had quickly ended.

He walked into the flames. The unnatural green fire rolled up his legs and touched him like a lover. He felt the fire's embrace as it chewed at his skin, but his body was powerful and resistant to heat.

This was why his children continued to feed the flame with chemicals and their bodies.

The Archon stepped farther into the heart of flames. They lashed at him, but his body remained.

He was strong.

Another step deeper in, and the flames embraced him, sucking the air away. Though he had no need, he took a breath.

Fire entered his lungs and burned him from the inside. He roared from the pain, for even gods knew misery. Another bulbous cronux came to the edge of the fire. It leapt forward, and as the flames touched its body, it burst.

The chemical waste inside its belly was used to bring down aircraft. It sprayed onto the Archon, and his flesh sizzled and popped as it charred and burnt away.

His muscles contracted and seared together as the flesh slid off. As he howled, no sound came. His tongue fell from his mouth to burn at his feet.

In the center of the flame, with the horrible pain, an odd peace grew as the flames melted his eyes and burned away his ears.

The Archon could not hear his children. The pain was so gripping that he was pulled from the hive mind. He existed only in this place, at this moment.

All else in the world quieted to him.

And there too was beauty.

He'd found it again.

Collapsed on the ground and overloaded with pain, the world was soft and silent.

Nothing hindered his mind or thoughts when he detached himself from the pain.

And though he had not come through his brother's gate, his mind reached toward it and beyond.

To the Mother.

Her love was warmer than flames. Her beauty carried weight beyond imagination.

And when she spoke, the words held the weight of the world.

My son.

She blessed him with the words.

But all at once, another thought came.

What if the weight of insanity had fallen upon him, and he only imagined her voice?

It didn't matter.

He knew that even as his stomach tissue burned away. He collapsed onto the ground.

The fire was greater than pain.

It was a womb, inside which he was becoming more.

With his fingers charred and cracked, he reached up into his back and dug in the nails. When he pulled forward, a sheet of flesh slid off and exposed the bare muscle.

He screamed, but the flames had burned away the tissues in his ear canals. He heard nothing.

But something moved in his back. Something deep within him parted between the muscles.

He was ascending.

He was becoming.

With that thought, the darkness took him again.

The Archon woke up sometime later—how long he didn't know—and found himself on the ground within the still-smoldering center of the building.

Tiny, crab-like cronux crawled around him and chewed off the dead skin, allowing a fresh layer to grow.

It had already begun.

His eyes had regrown, but they were blurry. As he blinked, old, damaged skin and tissue shed from his eye sockets. He stood, and the small cronux fell off him. He reached inside his mouth and pulled out a long, wet worm of a cronux and dropped it onto the ground. It had been inside him, digesting his ruined insides so he would grow back stronger.

Something flickered on his back.

Wings.

He stretched the long, leathery wings out to a massive span.

His children around him howled in praise and worship at his newfound beauty.

The fires of Moscow had burned him and damaged him, but he was now healed.

He was a god reborn.

And now...

He was ready to see his brother.

5

A SNAKE CRAWLED around in Endo's gut. Not a snake, but his intestines. When they were replaced, the doctor gave him tubes of tasteless gelatin and specific orders.

"Eat these every few hours, or the irritation might become unbearable."

The gelatin kept the artificial organs in a digestive cycle and prevented them from curling up.

Endo could feel the synthetic cable tucked inside his gut. It would pulse and slither as it worked through the digestion. And in his mind's eye, as it rubbed the inside of his stomach lining, the tissue became dark red and irritated as small cuts formed.

The miracles of medicine.

Who thought life was worth living if only to live in a constant state of suffering?

Endo had run out of his tasteless gel supplies days ago. He did his best to ration them, going as low as one a day. This tactic didn't remove the pain but lessened it.

He remembered looking at the last one, knowing it would provide relief but that it was only temporary.

Now he had to deal with the synthetic organs rubbing his stomach lining. The ridge tubing caught with each step he made.

Normal food could help, but it wasn't as smooth as the gelatin and didn't ease the process of his digestion.

All he could do to soften the pain was to remain still and focused on the road, though this was sometimes hard as they took unmaintained backroads. The bumpy ride was longer, but it helped them avoid threats and the catastrophe that fell on the Soviet Union.

But Endo felt every uneven road. Each bump sent a surge of pain through his body.

He did his best to focus on what was ahead.

That much was easy while in the front and on an open road, but often they would drive down wooded areas. Endo had to be attentive for anything prowling around in the dark.

Every time the road bended or the angle put the sun in their eyes, Endo imagined the enemy coming out of the woods and falling on them.

That's what he would do.

But these weren't men, were they?

They were demons.

And who knew how demons fought.

Endo hadn't seen one alive himself, but he had seen their tracks and had found a corpse.

The men from the truck stood around it, gawking and unsure of what to do. The dead four-legged beast had no eyes but teeth as thick as a fist.

They begged Endo to move on and leave it. They didn't see a purpose. They didn't know what to do.

Endo did. He pulled out his blade and opened up its chest. With his CAG gloves, he reached into its body.

There might come a time when he had to fight such a beast.

He wanted to know where the vulnerable parts were.

When he pierced an organ, a strange, milk-white fluid poured out, and black blood seeped from its veins, all strange and inhuman. Someone with a stronger expertise would have to find out what it was exactly.

But as Endo piled the creature's insides onto the dirt, he made a few observations.

No lungs.

Three hearts.

Several organs he couldn't classify.

If it breathed, Endo didn't know how. It didn't have eyes either, but from Endo's amateur inspection, the holes in its head could indicate a sensitivity to sound.

Though those were only theories.

One thing was clear. Endo glanced toward the trucks.

If they were attacked. . .

Few would survive.

The trucks were not armored, and the people were not fighters.

They settled on the long path.

Endo sat in the passenger seat of the lead truck as the convoy made its way to Berlin. It was silent. The drivers would switch out so each could take a rest, and none were in the mood to have a conversation. They stopped to change drivers. One man tipped his head to Endo and got out to sleep in the back. Endo was fine so long as he got to sleep for a short time here and there. He popped the clasps on his CAG helmet and set it beside him. He took a deep breath. It was nice to get real air from time to time. Maybe it could help with the pain if he could focus on his breathing.

All he wanted to do was get this convoy to a safe place and save as many lives as he could.

Why was he so desperate to help these people?

Endo didn't know.

He'd killed people just like them before, so why should he care for them? They weren't even Japanese.

They were Soviets.

The truck door opened, and Endo glanced over.

"Hey there, mate." The Englishman, Miles Westwood climbed into the driver's seat. "Suppose it's my turn behind the wheel."

Endo tipped his head.

He was always a man of few words.

Miles started up the truck and checked the mirrors, waiting for a signal from the other trucks that they were ready to move again. A moment later, he started off.

The sudden movements made Endo's intestines slither around. He let out a breath.

A few minutes passed in silence. Endo grabbed a bottle of water from a pack near his legs. They'd liberated supplies from a fuel station a few days before, but it was quickly running out. They'd have to find more.

They'd even picked up a few survivors, and some other vehicles had joined their convoy.

Endo hoped that they could—

"Been meaning to talk to you for a while now." Miles interrupted Endo's thought. "How'd a samurai end up in the Soviet Union?"

Endo looked at the Englishman. He'd never met a man like Miles. "I'm not a samurai. I'm a soldier."

Miles snorted. "Bit of a joke, mate."

Endo didn't respond.

"I suppose it was a shitty one."

Endo shifted his gaze away.

"Definitely shitty."

"Did you need to talk about something?" This might have been the most he'd talked in days.

"No, no, nothing too important."

Endo nodded and took another drink.

"I'm just good at reading people, you know?"

Endo flashed another look at Miles.

He doubted that.

Miles raised an eyebrow. "Don't believe me?"

"I'm afraid I don't." Endo put the cap back on the water bottle.

"I can tell you have a bug in your craw."

Endo was getting deeply tired with the conversation. "I don't know what that means."

"You're injured," Miles said with some sympathy, his hand still on the wheel. "Hard to tell since you keep so quiet and always wear that armor." He gestured toward Endo. "I can see something is chewing you up, though."

How had he given so much away? Endo had gone through years of training not to reveal pain or discomfort.

"How could you tell?" Endo asked.

Miles shrugged. "I have a knack for people. Used to work wonders for the ladies."

Endo considered for a moment. "I had my intestines replaced. I'm supposed to ingest a medicine that keeps the digestion functioning correctly. I ran out."

"Is it toraphin?" Miles winced and held out two fingers spaced apart. "Little tube of white jelly? Tastes like shit?"

The Englishman surprised Endo once more. "Yes, though it was tasteless."

"Ahh, it only looked like it tasted like shit, then. Never had it myself." Miles patted his stomach. "Me and my bits are all natural. No synthetics. There's probably a joke I could make in there, but you didn't seem to appreciate the last one, so I'll resist."

Endo almost laughed. Almost.

"Ahh, there we go. I see you." Miles pointed. "People love me. Well, at least until they get to know how much of a fucker I am. But generally speaking, I'm enjoyable company."

"I suppose."

"Actually, that bit about being all natural might be stretching the truth." Miles flashed a grin and pointed at his eye. "Forgot about this beauty."

Endo had noticed the man's two different colored eyes before, but he hadn't seen any reason to be concerned with it.

"Had to rip this bastard out and plug a new one in so I could get through the Soviet scanners and waddle around in this mess."

"Why?"

"Oh hell, I don't know, mate. Me and bad decisions are close friends. Typically, there's alcohol or a woman involved. Or both. But this time I made the decision sober. Was hoping to get the story on the aliens before everything turned tits up. But if I'm being honest with you, I'd probably have come anyway, because why not? Don't have anything better to do."

"You're a reporter?"

"I guess you don't recognize the name or face." He flashed a million-dollar smile. "I'm a reporter of a sort. The shitty, seedy kind anyway. Gets me into some interesting places. For example." He waved a hand at Endo. "Never met a samurai before."

Endo smirked and shook his head. "I told you. Only a soldier. Nothing more."

"At least you didn't call me racist for the joke."

"Why would I call you racist for the joke?"

Miles chuckled. "You don't get out much in the world, do you?"

When was the last time Endo had talked like this? Years ago, with his brothers of Three Raven. But he couldn't remember precisely when.

"We could do something about that pain," Miles said. "Toraphin isn't exactly easy to get, and it's not just straight gelatin or paste. I think if we hit another fuel station that isn't utterly ransacked, I could make a suitable enough substitute until we can find the real deal."

"Are you a doctor or a chemist?"

Miles raised his eyebrows. "No, not really, though I've slept with both a chemist and a doctor once. It wasn't at the same time." Miles glanced over at Endo. "Those sex jokes not landing? Bugger that, I guess I better move on to cock jokes."

Endo actually laughed now. It hurt his stomach, but it still felt good.

"Ahh." Miles grinned. "So it's cock jokes that are your thing."

6

A CONCERNED SURGEON rubbed his forehead with the back of his wrist.

Sweat stained his green medical gown.

Lei Zhao, Chairman and de facto leader of China, knew the scientist wasn't hot. He was in a secure room with temperature controls.

A man in a blue paper hospital gown was strapped down to a gurney in the sterile, white room. His vitals were hooked up to machines, which Zhao could read behind the three-inch-thick glass that separated him from the surgery.

"Tell him to begin," Zhao said, and the workers in the room scrambled to obey.

The surgeon wiped his forehead again. Hardly sanitary for the sterile room, but Zhao supposed he'd allow it under the circumstances.

The man on the gurney shuddered and pulled at his restraints.

Zhao watched keenly, for all of China balanced on the results.

He had been there when Beijing was overrun by bloody thirsty monsters. He watched it all from his tower. Mobs poured through the streets, and he wondered if this was how his predecessor felt when Zhao himself led a charge to overthrow the government.

Had that man watched the mobs flowing into the tower?

Had he felt the same razorblades of shame that Zhao felt?

Of course not. They had found the man cowering and blubbering, which he continued to do until they threw him off the roof.

Zhao would cower for no man or monster. He would stand and wait for death.

But Zhao's officers, in their traditional robes and garments, begged him, *"Please, sir, you have the mandate of heaven. You must lead us against the forces of Hell."*

With some reluctance, Zhao had gone with them to a waiting helicopter on the roof. And as he flew away, he saw a sea of blood and violence. His beloved city was being eaten alive.

Now was not his time to die. Not with so much work to do.

Not with so much more blood yet to be spilled.

He was spirited away to Hong Kong where he conducted military operations.

They amassed the largest military draft in Chinese history. Mobilizing men from every providence, town, and village.

But they would not be enough.

Every force near Beijing was sent against the monsters.

All were smashed.

First because of the monsters' strength.

Next because of the sheer tactical brilliance of the creatures.

The horrible creatures implemented new strategies and tactics unseen.

They were smart.

And their numbers grew.

A million men more would only be a million more lives to hand to those monsters. Zhao could see it now. He ordered his men that instead of aggressively retaking Beijing, they would now implement a strategy of containment.

They needed time to think.

But all the great military men amongst Zhao had few worthwhile ideas. They offered strategies and plans, but were still much the same.

Old ideas with new footing.

China hadn't fought a war in some time.

It showed with the incompetence of his officers.

But then Zhao's spymaster, Mr. Wu, spoke with him.

"Let me tell you about Alice Winters."

Zhao should have known better. Where strength fails, a keen mind prevails.

And that led him to this point.

Watching over a carefully conducted surgery in a sterile safe room.

A special forces group was able to bring down and capture several parasites.

Zhao had them.

One of them was in the room.

The surgeon walked over to the man on the gurney. He neatly rolled the sleeve of the blue gown as the man struggled and groaned.

Zhao stood at attention, hands clasped behind his back. He watched through the window, though video screens provided views from multiple angles.

The surgeon grabbed a scalpel. He wiped sweat from his face again and ran the blade down the man's bicep. The man screamed against his gag as the muscle exposed to the air and blood began to pour, darkening his blue gown.

With a crooked, nervous grin, the surgeon glanced back at the glass window.

The whole room sat quietly, waiting for Zhao's call.

But Zhao did not find it easy to speak. An unsettling feeling pressed down on his shoulders. A threshold stood before him, one that he alone could cross.

How simple life must be for all the other men in the room, the ones who simply waited to be told what to do.

Leadership, and the weight of decision, was a burden few could bear.

Such was the life of Lei Zhao.

He would do what others couldn't.

He tipped his head in confirmation.

The staff in the room spoke into the microphones.

"Proceed."

With the restrained man still thrashing against his restraints, the surgeon nodded. He pulled his tool cart a little closer to the gurney. Its wheels had an annoying squeak.

The surgeon retrieved a canister. He lifted it to eye level for examination before twisting the top on it and holding it close to the man's wound.

A cool mist poured out, as they kept it chilled to make things more manageable. Little wisps unfurled from the end.

The other man's eyes widened with fear, but Zhao had to wonder if the man could understand what they were doing and the purpose for it all.

They were trying to save China.

The wisps, slowly at first, lashed around the man's arm. Then a bulbous creature shaped like a tiny kidney poked out of the canister and nestled toward the man's wounds.

The man shrieked all the louder as the creature burrowed into the bloody wound.

The surgeon watched closely and set the canister down. He then turned to prepare the syringe on the table.

A syringe of cryo, just like Alice Winters had on Mars.

Just like the classified American reports said.

The wisps flailed outside the man's wound as it sank into his arm. The man jittered and shook.

The surgeon turned back to the man. His eyes opened in surprise as a wisp spun out and wrapped around his arm.

Zhao leaned in to watch things carefully.

The surgeon shrieked as he jerked backward, but the parasite pulled out of the other man's wound. Its wisps wrapped around the surgeon's arm and closed in more tightly.

A glance toward the man on the gurney, and Zhao saw he was seizing.

Panicking, the surgeon stumbled back as if he only needed to get distance from the parasite. But its wisps tightened, and it began to climb him like a ladder.

"You said it entered through wounds?" Zhao asked his spymaster, Wu, without taking his eyes from the room.

"That's what the American reports said." Wu's tone was mild and unconcerned, only curious.

The parasite ascended to the surgeon's face. The wisps pried his eyelids open and exposed the pink tissue underneath.

The frantic surgeon made the mistake of screaming. The wisps slid down his throat, and the parasite popped in between his teeth. Remaining wisps sucked in behind it like spaghetti noodles.

All at once, the surgeon began unnatural jerking movements. He snapped his head up and hissed, his eyes rolling back into his head.

It was disquieting to watch, but Zhao knew the importance of closer observation.

"I suppose it can enter other ways," he said. "How quickly did the American reports say they changed?"

"Ranging from minutes to the better portion of half an hour." Wu gestured toward the room. "This seems to be quite fast."

The surgeon whirled around the room as if he were drunk. Impossibly fast tentacles sprouted from his body, piercing through his skin as if it were a weak shirt seam.

His head jolted back and forth before he pressed his face to the window. He widened his mouth and hissed with bubbles of blood. The tip of his tongue fell out, as apparently he'd bitten his tongue off during the transformation.

The tentacles jabbed at the glass like spears.

Zhao flinched and took a step back, but he refused any other reaction. Such weakness in front of his men would lead to disaster.

"I have seen enough." Zhao held up his hand. "Clear it."

A lab assistant reached up and pushed a thick, orange button. The surgeon roared at the glass.

Fire jettisoned down from the edges of the ceiling to fill the room.

Zhao watched, holding his hand up. The surgeon thrashed about in the flames until he collapsed.

Even then, Zhao kept his hand raised for several seconds longer before lowering. The lab assistant released the button, and the fire stopped.

Zhao and Wu both stepped closer to peer through the glass.

The corpse was burnt beyond recognition. A black husk of burnt flesh.

Zhao looked at it carefully before speaking.

"We're going to need more volunteers."

Erkin Kahn had been a boy in a small town in Western China when the People's Army arrived. It had come in force, with armored trucks and men in uniforms with rifles. They told him they were Chinese, but Erkin was confused.

He too was Chinese, but he didn't look like the people in the army.

They were Han Chinese.

He was a Kasher.

For a time, things were fine, and as a child, he didn't really understand what was happening. The army built powerful structures that towered over the old buildings in Erkin's small town. New schools were built. The teachers were no longer Kasher, but Han, and they didn't speak Kashin, but Mandarin.

Erkin was given new books on the Mandarin language, and just like all the other students, he went to the playground where they built a fire from the Kasher language books.

He remembered laughing and jumping along with his friends as the books burned.

None of them had understood what was happening.

"You cannot speak Kashin at school anymore," his mother told him, shaking a finger at him. "Only at home. Only with us."

"But what if I don't know what to say?"

His mother grabbed him by the shoulders and pulled him close so she could stare into his eyes.

He still remembered the fear he saw in her.

"Then you say *nothing*, Erkin. You say *nothing*. Don't give them *any* reason."

Reason for what?

He was too young to understand.

Factories were built in his town, and he was ordered to work when his school closed. But though his time in school ended, Erkin kept studying. First in the few remaining Kasher books in his home, and then the books the army provided.

He was smart. Everyone knew it. He could stay up late reading and still arrive in time for his shift in the factory.

"Why do you read?" his friends would ask him. "What does it matter?"

Erkin always gave the same answer.

"I like to learn."

When his parents passed away, he collected the few remaining Kasher books they had and kept them in his new home. He read them over and over. Holy books, medical guides, tales of adventure, and more. He had no real preference. He read whatever was at hand.

It was nice to read in Kasher, but he read the Mandarin books the army handed out too.

Somehow those were less enjoyable.

After a few years, the army gave out IDs that had social credit ratings for their work in the factories and their obedience. If they achieved a good rank, they might be allotted more food or be allowed to marry.

Erkin worked hard and was given a full rating.

The rating allowed him to marry, and eventually he met a wife. They had a child—a baby girl.

She was seven years old when the army came for Erkin.

This time he was old enough to understand.

At first they claimed he had talked to a foreign journalist—he hadn't. Later he was told that *someone* had talked to a foreign journalist, and they ordered him to tell them who—but he didn't know.

A bag was placed over his head, and he was put into a truck.

The last he heard of his family was his daughter crying for him.

The truck drove for hours, and it became hard to breathe in the bag.

At some point, he passed out.

He was woken by a guard sometime later, and when he stepped out of the truck it was as he feared.

A re-education camp.

Guards patrolled inside the massive walls, and small, white buildings dotted each place.

Erkin had heard of this place. It was for criminals, for people who were a problem.

But Erkin was not. He could speak Mandarin better than anyone in his village. He pleaded his case to the processing officers.

"I have a full credit rating!" he said in Mandarin. "I haven't broken the rules!"

They were stunned by his fluency, but he was processed nonetheless.

They gave him a white shirt, white pants, and flimsy, green rubber shoes.

Erkin was there with a hundred or more other people. Some were Kashin from different villages, others looked like terrified Han Chinese but didn't speak Mandarin. There were more still who Erkin didn't recognize.

He hadn't eaten in more than a day, and he was filed into a cafeteria with a lot of other men. Erkin could tell those who were new, as they all looked up hopeless and confused. The ones who had been there a while knew what to do. They simply bowed their heads and ate the food out of a bowl with their hands.

Erkin looked down at his bowl. In it was some kind of green paste he'd never seen. He'd never eaten with his hands before, but his stomach still rumbled. As he was getting ready to take his first scoop, two guards showed up. They grabbed him and demanded he come with them.

The guards piled Erkin into a cold room and stood in the corner.

A Han Chinese man was sitting behind a table. A lit cigarette smoldered in his hand, and he watched Erkin beyond small, pop-bottle glasses.

"Have a seat," he said.

Erkin scratched his neck and glanced at the guards who loomed behind him.

He took a seat.

The man pulled out an ID card, and Erkin recognized his face on it. It was the card they took from him.

The man plugged the card into a tablet reader and scrolled through the documents.

Erkin didn't know what his file said. He'd never been allowed to read it.

"You speak Mandarin?" the man asked.

Erkin nodded.

"Why are you here, Mr. Kahn?" The man never took his eyes from the screen.

"I don't know," Erkin said earnestly. "There was some mistake. I shouldn't be here."

"We do not make mistakes. Perhaps *you* have made a mistake." The man looked up then, casting a dark glance at Erkin over his glasses.

Erkin went quiet.

The man let out a breath and set the tablet down. He slid out Erkin's card and placed it into his pocket. "My name is Mr. Wu. I will be asking you some questions." He puffed his cigarette but didn't look away. "Answer everything."

Erkin nodded.

A trail of smoke swirled up from Wu's cigarette. "What are you?"

Erkin was confused. "I... I am..."

Wu studied him. "I am Chinese. What are you?"

"I'm Kasher."

Another long pause followed as cigarette smoke snaked into the air.

"And do you pray?" Wu asked.

Erkin's chest clenched. His shoulders pulled in and his back slumped. He wanted to squeeze into a ball. "*I do,*" he whispered.

"Do you pray for Chairman Zhao? Do you pray for his health?"

The tension in Erkin's chest grew tighter still. "*I do,*" he lied.

Wu leaned forward and pointed with the cigarette. "*I don't believe you. A man who would say he is Kasher and not Chinese is a traitor in time.*"

"No, no!" Erkin shook his head. The powerful hands of the guards slammed down on his shoulders, holding him to his seat.

Wu put a finger on the tablet. "These reports say you are smart. You are highly fluent in Mandarin. More so than any other *Kasher* I've met. A *smart* man could be useful to Chairman Zhao. A *smart* man could be trusted to guide his community in the right direction and to root out traitors."

With some reluctance, Erkin nodded.

Wu stared at him, his gaze heavy. It squeezed the breath from Erkin's chest. "Then give me three names. Three traitors." He held up fingers. "*Three*, and we can talk about what happens next."

Three traitors? Erkin didn't know any. There had been riots in the factory and bad talk behind closed doors, but traitors? He couldn't name anyone.

"I don't know any traitors."

Wu's face remained flat and unreadable. He reached under his chair and pulled up a book. He dropped it right in front of Erkin. "I know of one," he said.

It was one of Erkin's books. A medical book in Kashin.

The bookmark still held his place.

"This, and others, were found when we searched your house," Wu said. He plugged the cigarette into his mouth and took a deep drag. The end sizzled red. Wu pulled it out and exhaled. "You do not love China. You do not surrender traitors. You keep illicit goods. You are three times a traitor. You will remain here until you learn obedience and loyalty, or you will be shot."

"No, no, I—" Erkin moved from the seat but the guards pressed down on him. They pulled his arms back, and one slid a hand in front of his mouth, muffling him. They shoved him down. His face flattened painfully against the table as they pressed the back of his skull.

"A party member has already been dispatched to live with your wife and daughter. They will be inspected for loyalty and taught obedience. And in time—"

The thought sent fire through Erkin's chest. He lost himself. He screamed and struggled, but they pressed even harder against the table.

"—you will learn loyalty."

7

WHEN DOCTORS ATTACHED Alice's new arm, it felt cold and dead. They connected the modules to nerve endings, which sent signals to her brain when the synthetic skin touched something.

The arm tricked her brain into thinking she had real skin.

That it was still human.

Everything had been so uncoordinated. At times, something as easy as lifting Eli was a chore that made her collapse into tears.

But she got through it with training.

She was at the gym six days a week lifting weights, struggling to rebuild her body.

She remembered the pain.

The sweat.

Her cheeks were red and her breathing ragged as she stared into the mirror and curled weights.

The pain made her nauseated as the nerve endings struggled with confusion and her body tried to coordinate.

But she never gave in. She made each session and kept at it to the point where she could, at times, forget her arm was gone and that something mechanical with chips and microfibers was attached to her body.

The more time she put into it, the more pain she invested and the harder she struggled...

The stronger she became.

So too was it with the hive mind.

Each time she stepped out of the drop cage was one more rep.

Each time she lifted her hand and grabbed ahold of the creatures within the hive mind, her body and mind hardened.

And each time she curled her fingers and broke their wills, she became stronger.

Deadlier.

But she thought again of the synthetic skin layered over her hand, there to trick the brain.

To make the arm believe it was still human.

Alice wondered what that all meant to her as she took a breath, one that may not be necessary.

Still, she exhaled and took another.

It made her feel human.

A muscle twitched in her side, and the sensation reminded her of the wisps sliding around beneath her skin. It was as if the parasite, for whatever reason, had begun to move again—like it had come back to life.

Even now, sitting in the dark hull of a dropship speeding through Soviet airspace, she envisioned the edges of the wisps sliding between her muscles and digging into her body.

She took a breath and tried to focus.

If she settled her nerves and calmed her breathing, she imagined the wisps wiggling into her lungs.

But she couldn't think of that now, not with all that was happening.

The Janissary was out there. A long-limbed monster wise enough to shroud himself in the dark void of the hive mind. Though she'd never seen him, she'd touched him in the hive mind and from that, she knew him.

She could see him in her mind's eye, like a player across the board of a game of chess, but she didn't know where he was.

The Archon had moved on. She couldn't feel him in the hive mind at all, but she would find him in time. For now, though, she needed to keep her focus on the Janissary.

He was dangerous, not just in words or actions. . .

But feelings.

He had a warm embrace and a gentle, welcoming touch. She could sense him sometimes coming close to her mind, feeling him rub the edges. She was in such torment and disarray, and he would whisper.

Let us in.

And sometimes Alice wondered. . .

What if I did?

Would the world be so bad if she let him inside?

Why was she afraid of what he could show her?

But then the same question always came to her.

What about Eli?

Her son. He'd already lost so much.

Could he lose his mother too?

Focus. Don't let the monsters in.

Alice had the sudden desire to breathe real air. She popped the clasps on her CAG helmet. The few strands of blonde hair that weren't tied back fell in front of her face as she set the helmet aside.

The red interior light of the ship shined down on her face. Soldiers lined the docking benches, and they all turned when she took her helmet off.

None of them spoke in anything louder than a whisper, or if they did, they did it on closed communication.

Alice didn't need to hear them. She could tell by the angle of their heads as the internal red lights of the ship blinked.

Their eyes were always on her.

Always waiting.

And they were thinking.

Is she even still human?

Alice supposed, at this point, that was all just a matter of opinion.

She caught the eyes of one Soviet soldier.

He looked away.

They were afraid of her—afraid of what she could do.

She wasn't like them. She wasn't a soldier.

But the world didn't need another soldier.

It needed a monster.

When the red light began to blink, Alice snatched her helmet and placed it on her head. She took her position inside a drop cage.

The cage wasn't like the others on the ship. Soviet engineers had altered it to fit her CAG.

The first time Alice ever dropped, her heart pounded in her chest at the frantic horror of feeling totally out of control.

Not this time.

Even as the cage's release doors opened and her cage loosed into the air, her vital readouts remained consistent. Alice was of such a clear mind she could hear her own breathing inside the helmet.

Grand Marshal Garin wanted to retake Warsaw, but it was Alice who picked the drop this time. She didn't even know the name of the town. She'd only felt the pull.

There was a Harbinger here.

"The Archon has come as ruler of the world," she'd told Garin. *"The Janissary controls his armies. But the Harbingers are the ones that hold the horde together and keep them from splintering. Kill them, and we'll tear the horde apart."*

Town by town, mile by bloody mile, they would roll the Janissary's influence back. Cut him apart, chase him into a corner, and give him no room to breathe.

Alice had come to steal his breath.

The dropship landed them in the center of the city, and Alice came out of the cage with her hand raised, like some war witch on the field of battle. The creatures came and they died, and there was little else to speak of.

Rain pattered her armor, and Alice held her fist in the air. She screamed inside her helmet, which felt so tight she peeled it off and dropped it into the mud.

All around her were explosions and gunfire. Her team called out orders as the red soldiers rushed around her, taking cover.

But not Alice. No, she walked down the center of the broken pavement, her feet leaving prints where the mud had bubbled up. Fires crawled up the buildings and the smell of burning flesh filled the air. People screamed in the distance, but Alice found her focus in the madness. She walked on two planes of existence.

They came for her. First the once-men, mewing and moaning with hunger. A crowd of dozens, but it didn't matter.

She cut them apart with her will, and just like many times before, they turned upon each other.

Eyeless cronux came, crawling out of the buildings. They opened their thick jaws and displayed their jagged teeth.

She could feel them, and she knew that they could already taste her. As she closed her fist once more, she broke their wills. They collapsed or stood their ground dumbly as the Soviet soldiers let loose a barrage of bullets.

A cronux near her had its head pulped with several well-placed shots. Another dragged out in a circle like dumb beast before catching a spray of bullets and turning over dead.

More creatures came, more died, and through it all, Alice walked the field.

They were nightmares, but she was the dreamer.

This was her world.

She took a moment to pause as three soldiers moved up on a creature, blasting rounds into its belly. A flame trooper scorched it, and the creature's skin sizzled and cracked.

This too was not much to speak of.

She'd done this before.

She'd do it again.

Alice and her team were a machine. They rolled through so quickly she could practically hear the *click-click-click* of their gears turning.

Alice led them toward the Harbinger over the broken bodies of the dead and the dying. They carved a hole through the once-men. The dumb beasts continued to struggle with each other as flame troopers moved past, scorching them.

Alice paid them no mind.

"There." She pointed at a bald patch of ground where the mud was thick. Wet strands of hair stuck to her face. *"Come."* She spoke in both this world and the other.

As if on command, the Harbinger rose from the ground with mud dripping off his powerful frame.

"Take it, take it!" a Soviet soldier shouted. He shoved Alice's helmet into her hands.

Without peeling her eyes from the monster, she put the helmet on her head. It sank down and connected with a hiss. Internal fans and environmental systems switched on to compensate for the moisture on her head.

The Harbinger was strong. Alice couldn't break his will, but that wasn't her plan.

The soldiers were there.

Through the darkness, with the glow of the burning fires and with the rain falling on them, the soldiers fanned out and fired weapons upon the Harbinger.

This wasn't like Felicity, where they weren't properly armed or prepared. These soldiers had capable weapons and cutting-edge CAG.

The bullets peppered the Harbinger and broke his armor hide.

Alice only watched.

The Harbinger's tentacles flailed and reached, but the soldiers stayed back and took cover with tactical maneuvering.

There was a loud *thunk* as a soldier shot a rocket-propelled grenade and blew off the Harbinger's leg. Another *thunk* and the explosion impacted the Harbinger's chest. A third with a series of rifle shots blew off a large portion of the Harbinger's back and made the tentacles drop.

The Harbinger collapsed, and more shots peppered his hide.

But he wasn't fighting anymore.

He was whispering to Alice.

"Come." He beckoned her within the hive mind. *"Come."*

Alice stepped forward.

The Soviets shouted at her to stop, but they couldn't understand. She felt the Harbinger and knew how weak he was.

There was no threat.

She closed in. Rain peppered the Harbinger's face. A fold of skin, like hide armor, peeled off his head, and Alice could see the almost human face beneath.

His cheeks were sunken in, and his eyes were deep set, like a half-starved corpse.

He spoke now in the real world. *"We offer. . . a deal."* His words were strained, as if it were painful for him to speak. *"Come to us. . . Choose who lives . . . Choose who dies."*

Alice popped the clasps on her helmet and lifted it.

The rain pelted her, but she didn't mind.

This was the first time she'd ever spoken to one like this, and she wanted to look the bastard in the eyes. "I'm going to kill every one of you. No matter how long it takes, and no matter where I have to go."

The Harbinger's wet, rubbery skin slid into something that might have been a smile.

Perhaps he'd met the extent of his abilities to speak.

Or maybe he only wanted her to hear.

Your son.

He spoke within the hive mind.

We'll come and take your son.

Alice felt the words like a punch in the stomach. She was forced to take a step back.

We already speak to him. He's already ours.

"Kill him!" Alice shouted at the flame soldier. "Burn his goddamn face off!"

The flame soldier stepped up and leveled his weapon. A burst of flame splashed across the Harbinger's face, making the skin crackle and open as it cooked.

But the Harbinger smiled and whispered one last time.

If we can't take you. . . then we'll take him.

He grinned until the fire burned his lips away.

A sudden and intense pain flooded over Alice, making her wince and nearly collapse.

Something shifted within the hive mind, like a massive weight moving from a scale.

It wasn't the Harbinger's death.

It was something else.

Blood dripped out of her nose and down her lip. She dabbed her finger into it.

What did it mean?

A moment of silence passed as the rain poured down on the burning Harbinger.

The Soviets all stood still, their armor dark with mud and blood.

"What now?" one of the soldiers asked, his voice buzzing over the CAG's external speakers.

Alice looked down at the Harbinger. The rain rolling down her face mixed with the blood.

What was that? A sudden quake within the hive mind? A disconnect?

Was something hiding?

"Winters?" the man repeated. *"What now?"*

She looked at her bloody fingers and then at the man.

"I don't know."

8

THE JANISSARY WAS NOT like the Archon or a Harbinger. His body was not meant for conflict. He was frail by comparison. His limbs were long and slim. He did not have claws, but slender, flexible fingers.

He was not built for battle but for thought and consideration.

Careful planning.

He was old in the ways of war and an aged veteran of the Mother's ambitions.

He understood conflict and struggle.

But this war was different.

Alice Winters.

He knew the name, even if he didn't quite understand why she had it or how she'd gotten it.

The Janissary had faced many dangerous opponents, but never one like her.

Never an enemy within.

This was a new war. A new kind of battle.

It required new tactics.

Such was the reason for his existence.

He began by splitting his forces into many small squads and harrying the cities. It had become difficult, as all those that could easily be taken were already drawn in. Now all that remained were the people who hid in dark corners.

The Janissary's forces dragged them out.

Within his mind's eye, he saw them break down doors and enter homes, fighting room to room as they picked clean the bones of each city.

But Alice Winters was killing too many of his forces. And with the gate down, it was now impossible to get more warriors in.

He had to wait for the Archon to take another gate.

It was important, though, to keep Alice Winters distracted.

He had to devise a new plan.

That's why he was here, beneath a gray sky and looking out upon the ocean.

The Janissary stepped onto a beach, and sand filled between his toes. At his side, dark acolytes stood, their heads bowed in devotion and purpose, their minds weaving with his for control of the horde.

Near him, an army of servants watched the hallowed procession.

The Janissary walked ahead of them all, his narrow feet leaving thin impressions in the sand. He glided to the lapping water and knelt down. All the servants behind him held still, as he immersed his hand and raised it.

Water ran between his thin, pointed fingers.

The Janissary stood up and cast his gaze across the endless blue. He'd grown eyes just for this purpose.

He wanted to know the world as Alice Winters knew it.

He wanted to see what she saw, to understand her and her ways.

He'd given up a Harbinger. Alice Winters thought it was to carry a message to her in her own language, but that was not its only purpose.

It was a distraction.

Just as Alice Winters was filling her mind with war, the Janissary was stretching his out to all the eggs grown here in the world—the *chimera*. Cronux that looked human.

The Archon had used chimera to infiltrate Leningrad and tear it apart, but they had been used sparingly since.

Now was the time.

Alice Winters could possibly detect the beings within the hive mind, so the Janissary focused his mind and reached out to grab all the thin, little strands that connected his mind to theirs. He pulled them taunt.

He gave one order.

Go.

Then he shredded the strands.

It was a violent burst that all felt within the hivemind. The Janissary himself felt a sharp blade of pain within his head.

He would not know where the chimera were or how effective they had been.

But they would be moving quietly.

Unseen.

No longer part of the hive mind.

But that was only one front of the Janissary's war.

He had been holding council with one of Alice Winters's own.

Her son.

With his mother so far away, her son was all alone. The Janissary had sensed him. A confused and lonely little boy.

The Janissary had gone in with the same warm and gentle touch Alice Winters had refused, and he offered it to the boy.

And the boy took it.

The Janissary showed him what little he had seen and known of the human world. The places they had gone. The sights excited the boy.

Then there was but one question to ask.

Where is your home?

And the boy, living with such uncertain gifts and understanding, had whispered back.

America.

It was somewhere across the sea.

"*Worm.*" The Janissary used human words as he turned back to his servants. Language was still a new thing for him, but he was a fast learner.

The great beast sauntered forward, barking into the air, for it was a strong but dumb thing.

The Janissary looked to his acolytes standing attentively and awaiting his orders.

And with his cold, harsh voice, he spoke in the real world once more. *"Now."*

They turned toward Worm, and though the Janissary did not have claws, his acolytes did. Not for war, but for the gift of transformation.

They came to the side of Worm and cut into him.

Worm jerked and howled in pain, though he did not resist.

He knew and understood.

After the acolytes cut him deeply, he slithered in half. A new face was already growing inside the wound.

One beast had become two.

The first beast understood its purpose, even without command. It slithered onto the beach and into the lapping water.

The Janissary watched until Worm sank below and could no longer be seen. Then the other approached and did the same.

Alice Winters could fight so boldly because she fought upon enemy ground, with people dying that she cared nothing for.

The Janissary would change things.

He would bring the war home for Alice Winters.

The cronux were a race fueled by evolution.

Ever changing.

Ever improving.

Always evolving.

Niklas Koch wasn't a cronux. He'd simply been a man. He had lived in East Germany, and several times a week, he had crossed the border into West Germany for day labor.

Niklas had been poor and starving, but not a moron. The West Germans didn't need the labor. They did it for humanitarian purposes.

The West Germans were sympathetic to the East. They were the same people.

All that separated them was a wall.

Niklas had been granted a worker pass, and he would cross the border to do simple factory work. He enjoyed the work, even if it was the Soviet Union that collected his wages and dolled him out only a portion. It was still a bigger slice than some got, and he could afford to feed his family.

But Niklas Koch wasn't feeding his family anymore.

He was dead.

One of those unfortunate few who got caught in the swarm. But unlike others, he hadn't been mangled and infested with parasites. No, screaming and clawing at the dirt, he'd been dragged into the dark corner of some building where a horrible, massive creature bit off his head.

That had been where the story of Niklas Koch came to an end and another took its place.

A Harbinger chewed his brain and puked it into a chimera egg. Then something grew that could wear Niklas's face as a mask.

And now that chimera was waiting in line with the refugees at the border of Germany.

While the large wall was still there, the guards who would shoot people fleeing in or out were not.

Perhaps they too were all dead.

"Pass! Show us your pass!" A West German guard shouted at the refugees crowding the gate.

There were other borders and other places. The chimera's brothers may well be there too, but he was here and in line.

Unlike his brothers of a generation or more before, the newest brood had changed.

Improved.

Evolved.

He breathed with short, panicked breath, mimicking the way the humans around him had.

"Papers!" a guard demanded. "Show us your papers!"

Few had their papers, and the lines of refugees only stretched farther and farther.

But the West Germans were sympathetic to their brothers. They spoke the same language, shared a common culture.

They were one people.

Niklas Koch had known this.

The chimera that now wore Niklas's face also knew it.

The gates were opened, and guards maneuvered the refugees into processing locations.

The chimera stayed with the crowds and left the Soviet Union.

He now entered into the European Federation.

9

ELI WAS FIVE YEARS OLD, but his birthday was coming up within the next few months.

"I'm five and a half."

That was his preferred answer when adults asked about his age. Not that he exactly understood what "half" meant, but it did make him sound older.

There were a lot of things he didn't understand fully, and these days, he understood even less.

Why did he now live in the White House? Why did he have men with his family all the time? Why was it that he only saw Grandma Cora and not his mother?

What were the whispers in his head?

Sometimes they were soft and quiet, like the volume had been turned low on the TV. Other times it was as if they were in the same room.

But they were always there and strange in a way that Eli couldn't explain. They weren't speaking with words, but he understood what it meant.

They didn't hurt, but they weren't exactly comfortable either.

How could they be when it was like someone was over his

shoulder whispering while he was trying to watch TV or look at a book? It was even hard to sleep, but did that even matter?

He hadn't slept in days. He wasn't tired, though, and he really didn't mind lying in his bed for hours and hours.

It was fine.

But last night wasn't.

Last night he stared at the ceiling. The whispers had been low and quiet all day, but all of a sudden they got louder as they chittered in his ear.

Oh, he wished they would just be quiet and just let him sleep, even if he didn't really have to anymore.

First, they just asked questions.

Then they made demands.

Eli only listened.

Every morning, he would pretend to sleep when Grandma Cora came in to wake him. The one time he told her he hadn't slept at all, she got upset.

He knew it was bad to lie, but his preschool teacher had explained something to him after he'd made a friend cry. He'd only told the girl her drawing was ugly.

"It's not nice to always say what you think when it makes people upset," the teacher had said.

He decided he wasn't going to tell Grandma Cora everything.

He didn't like to see her upset.

The next morning, Grandma Cora came in smiling and already dressed. "Wake up, sweetie, time for us to go get breakfast."

"Grandma? Where do we live?"

She grinned. "The White House now. Your grandpa is president, so we have to sleep here."

"Who are the men who go with us?"

She gestured for him to get up. "Sweetie? Come on, we have to go eat."

"Who are they?" Eli repeated.

"Oh." She smoothed her dress with her hands. "They just make sure we're safe, that's all."

"How many of them are there?" Eli's voice started to crack.

Grandma Cora's smile faded. "You don't need to bother with that. Why do you want to know?"

Eli sat up on his bed. "They asked me, Grandma. They want to know where I am."

Grandma Cora's eyes widened, and when she spoke, she did so slowly. "Eli, why are you being so silly? Who asked you that?"

Eli watched her for a moment. Was she upset?

Was this one of the times when he shouldn't tell her?

Then the whispers came back. First as a rumble, and then they grew. He twisted his head away from Grandma Cora as he listened to them. There were no words exchanged between them, only an understanding.

"The monsters, Grandma. They wanted to know."

Eli couldn't help it. A smile slipped across his face. They might be monsters, but their touch was warm and comforting. It wasn't at all like the confusion he felt here.

"And they're coming to meet me."

10

JOHN WINTERS STOPPED in front of a mirror and inspected his suit. He had to imagine that President Warren had a person on staff to check his damn suit, but after cleaning house, John was running on a skeleton crew as they worked to rebuild the team.

Reports were coming in about a breakout in China, and as Roles put it:

"Beijing popped."

But the Chinese were a secretive people, and what little info did get through couldn't be trusted. There were some who would be applauding the collapse of the Chinese nation, but not John.

The Chinese weren't a people he often agreed with, but their government drew more than a billion people out of starvation and poverty.

John often defined his political doctrine as a pursuit of the least amount of misery.

China not starving to death was a step in the right direction, all other things aside.

After the news about Beijing, John gave his chief of staff an order.

"Call in the Chinese ambassador."

But dealing with the Chinese was no easy feat. They were an

insular people, and while past diplomats adhered to a strategy of quiet compliance, the new generation, with ambitions of honor and wealth, were dubbed Wolf Warrior diplomats.

They were aggressive and assertive, and prideful to a fault.

Still looking into the mirror, John adjusted his tie and with McAndrews at his side, he entered the room with the Chinese ambassador. They had opted to keep the meeting small because of the sensitive nature.

But if things were going badly in China, the ambassador didn't show it. He was a young, neatly dressed Han Chinese man with just a hint of a smile on his face. He wore stylish, gold-framed glasses and had a male secretary standing just to his left despite an open seat being available.

John was sure the ambassador was the son or nephew of someone important.

McAndrews eyeballed the standing secretary and half whispered to John, "You're not going to make me stand, are you?"

"No." He gestured toward a seat for McAndrew and took one himself. "Good afternoon. Thank you for coming."

The ambassador straightened in his seat and raised his chin, a hint of suspicion in the air. "Of course. Typically the first meeting between our nations with a new president is done with a great deal more fanfare." His smile widened, showing off perfectly set, white teeth. "President Warren treated me to an elegant meal. It's unfortunate how he died." He spoke in perfect English.

John didn't flinch. He wasn't about to let a man half his age get under his skin.

"These are informal times, Ambassador, and I'm afraid I'm not as elegant of a showman as President Warren was."

"But why have you summoned me, Mr. President?"

John decided to be blunt. "We've heard about the trouble in China."

The ambassador gave nothing away. "What of it?"

John exhaled. He hated the little games in politics.

"The Soviets opened up a gate to another world and caused the collapse of Moscow. Now the entire Soviet Union is on the threat of collapse. They only survived with American aid."

The ambassador chuckled quietly and removed his frames, folded them, and slid them into his jacket pocket. "With American aid?" He mocked a confused look. "And here I suspected that the Soviet's long-running and perfectly functioning rail system was upset by Americans. It seems it became dysfunctional at precisely the moment the Soviets most needed it. How inconvenient."

John folded his hands on the table. "If you're so well-informed, then you would know that Grand Marshal Sergi Garin was harried into Berlin and requested support from America and the European Federation. We provided assistance that stopped the destruction of that city."

"Ahh, *Major General* Sergi Garin." The ambassador refused to use Garin's assumed rank. "You see, I haven't met that man. I did meet *General Secretary Durak Suka-Blyat* before he perished in Moscow. He was a man I knew, a man I trusted. . . but Major General Garin, who requested your support?" Still grinning, the ambassador tightened his eyes. "I don't know this man."

"Ambassador, I'm not here to play games. Not with the world at risk. We know the situation in China is expanding."

"Mr. President, I'm not sure you should be so concerned with what happens in China. Haven't you only assumed office because so many of your predecessors were killed? What about the Comanche with nerve gas on your southern border or the talk of a second American Civil War?" The ambassador leaned his elbows on the table. "I think you have far too many problems of your own to be concerned with China."

John felt an itch in his throat. He often got that when he wanted to scream.

"I understand the position of both countries, but we want to provide aid in any capacity to help with the matter."

"Assistance?" The ambassador's smile faded. "America has done nothing but sit across a distant ocean and lambast China on how we should run our affairs. Or did you forget the sanctions you placed over the fabricated Kasher camps? Or the propaganda lies you spread about our people and our way of life." The ambassador shook his head. "We do not seek your assistance, nor do we trust you. China will do as it always has done. It will see to itself." The hint of a smile returned.

John could have him thrown out of the country. It'd create an international incident, but he could do it. With one phone call, this man, his family, and his entire staff could be expelled.

But the smirking ambassador knew he wouldn't do it.

John was in a weak position. An untested leader walking on shaky ground.

He knew it, and the ambassador knew it.

But John was angry.

"Ambassador?" John fought to keep his voice calm. "Have you ever killed anyone?"

The ambassador shifted and glanced at his secretary. "No, I haven't."

"I have. Did it with a rifle." John's eyes were hard as he stared at the man.

The ambassador didn't blink.

"It wasn't easy," John went on. "We had to crawl through hell to get there, but when we did, I lined him up in my sights and pulled the trigger. You know what happened next?"

The ambassador shook his head, his eyes widening. "I don't see how any of this is—"

"I aimed for the next one, and the one after that, and the one after that." John folded his hands in front of himself. His words felt cold. "Men who've never been to war should not casually dismiss the concerns of those who have. I'm a serious man, with serious concerns and I will not be talked to with disrespect. Whatever has gone on between our countries pales in comparison with what could happen. Believe me. I know what a pile of bodies looks like. Do you?"

The ambassador stared back at him.

"Ninety five percent of the Soviet Union is under siege. If we can't get together and get these things on hand, it'll spread across the world and we'll have an *Earth siege*. See that Chairman Zhao hears of our offer of assistance. I look forward to communicating with him directly to see where we can help." John rose from his seat, and McAndrews stood with him. He took his language seriously and rarely used profanity. "Now get the fuck out of my house."

But there were times for exceptions.

The ambassador said nothing else as John and McAndrews left the room.

MARAT HAD MADE a lot of bad decisions in his life—most of them being in the last few weeks, of course.

But not simply agreeing but *requesting* to go back into Moscow with Moller may have been the worst decision—the cherry on his cat turd of a life.

"You don't have to go, Marat. I know you're not a soldier," Moller said before they left.

But with an American cigarette dangling from his lips and a pretty blonde girl looking him in the eyes, he felt like Superman from one of the smuggled American comics he used to read—a Superman who smokes, has synthetic lungs, and is poorly equipped for all forms of combat.

Oh, and he didn't fly either.

"No, no. You don't know base. I know base. I am only one who knows base," he said.

"We brought the gate down in Felicity before by amping power into it. We could try it again."

"American system is not like the Soviet. American is very technical. We are an art form."

He tried to explain it to her, but it was hard to explain. The Americans built their systems in very *formal* and technical ways, but the Soviets were far more intuitive and creative within the guidelines. It was why they always had the better hackers.

A college instructor had said it best when he explained it to Marat.

"You have to learn to make love to the system. Caress it like a beautiful woman."

The man had closed his eyes and made sickening gestures. Marat had only scowled in horror and never asked the man any questions in private again.

"We make love to system," he said to Moller, and made those same similar hand gestures, though he tried his best to be more tasteful with it.

She nodded, but if she really understood what the hell he was talking about, he didn't know. Either way, she agreed he needed to go. An American engineer, an expert or not, simply wouldn't understand Soviet systems.

Oh, it was such a struggle to explain things. He was trying to smooth out his English, and he hoped it was getting better. Some of those shitty English lessons back from high school and college were coming back to him.

"I before E except after C," he remembered his language teacher telling him.

Fifteen-year-old Marat had raised his hand and asked, *"How about the word foreign?"*

Everyone in the class laughed, and Marat had grinned as the teacher got angry.

Thinking of that now, he grimaced. Why had everyone laughed? It wasn't even funny.

Was he really so stupid as a teenager?

The answer was, of course, yes, and another unfortunate truth was that he was still stupid.

At least he was aware of it now.

Before she left, Moller told him to spend the next few days preparing.

He looked her right in the eyes, and with the most serious face he could manage, he nodded, as if to suggest he was already forming a plan for what needed to be done.

In reality, he spent most of the time crying and looking up internet porn, which was an exciting thing indeed for a man born within the censor-heavy land of the Soviet Union.

Though the pornography was certainly a good distraction, Marat found his eagerness to enter into hell for a pretty blonde fade a little each day.

The strange part was his ability to choose. Choices made things complicated. Certainly Marat had some control of his life in the Soviet Union, but there were other times where the choices were stripped from his hands. Great punishments were offered for disobedience.

So when his choices were, "Do this or get shot in the head," he really didn't have much of a choice at all.

It was at his last doctor's appointment that everything really hit him.

The doctor looked up from some scans. "Have you been smoking?"

"Meh." Marat raised his hand and waved the doctor off, which resulted in a long, bitchy lecture from a man far more educated and wealthy than Marat ever would be.

If he wanted to, he could lean back in the chair, stare the doctor in the eyes, and say, "Eat shit, fat beef."

He had told someone on the base to *"Eat shit, fat beef,"* but they seemed more confused than insulted. He supposed the expression only really worked in Ukrainian and didn't translate well.

But again, if he so chose, he could tell this doctor to eat shit and walk out.

That idea had a strange feel to it.

Of course, there would be some repercussions. He wasn't a citizen of the West, for sure, but he wasn't going to be executed either way.

He had some small freedoms in life that he'd never had before. He was free to tell a doctor to *eat shit, fat beef,* even if the man didn't understand what any of that meant. He was free to smoke cigarettes, despite ruining his expensive, new lungs

And he was free to decline re-entering the Soviet Union.

He imagined standing in front of Moller, a lit cigarette in his mouth—because he always felt cooler with a cigarette in his mouth— and telling her how he really felt.

"Actually, the alien business can all fuck off, I don't owe the Soviet Union anything. But you're beautiful, and I'm told American women like accents. How about I show you how skilled of a lover I am?"

Of course, in his imagination, he spoke English far clearer than could realistically be expected. And he was also pretty sure when hearing the rumors of American women's love for accents, they weren't talking about broken Ukrainian.

He decided he wouldn't tell the doctor to fuck off, and he went to his last appointment before heading into the Soviet Union.

The doctor had asked him again if he was still smoking.

Marat nodded. The doctor went into his rant again, but Marat barely heard him.

He was thinking of that very first day when the gate opened. When he watched friends and coworkers die.

He couldn't imagine what the place looked like *now* with the gate in there and opened so long.

He shivered.

"See? See these side effects? It's important to stop smoking or you may get more of these shivers," the doctor berated him.

Marat smiled politely and nodded again.

When the doctor's lecture ran out of steam, Marat headed to his room to queue up the internet once more for an hour or so of brain-fogging porn. But on the way, a weight settled onto his shoulders. He stopped between buildings and leaned against a wall as he lit another cigarette. He didn't even really want one at the moment, but why the hell not? He had some small measure of freedom now, but were his hands really so tied before?

He hadn't known the gate was going to open in Moscow, but he hadn't done anything to stop it either. What could he have done? Stayed and turned it off? *Maybe*, but the whole damn thing lit up by itself. Who's to say their controls would even continue to work?

No, there were no heroics for Marat at that moment.

When things went to Hell, he did what he did best.

He ran.

"*Fuck*." A tinge of guilt ran down his back. He rubbed a hand through his hair and shook his head.

His English may be poor, but at least the F-word was always an effective tool for how he felt.

He looked at his smoldering cigarette.

This was an American brand. He'd have to pay good money for smuggled American cigarettes in the Soviet Union, but here in the U.S., they practically handed them out to children and even put fun, little cartoon characters on the front.

Marat's pack had a sexy-looking tiger woman on the front.

He still had most of the pack too.

Oh, freedom came with a lot of things. He had the freedom to sit on his ass, watch internet porn, and smoke the rest of this pack of sexy, tiger-woman cigarettes.

Or.

He could throw the pack down, get his shit together, and go into Moscow because Moller needed him and like it or not, he was responsible for what happened.

"Fuck," he said, still staring at the cigarette.

He flicked it to the ground and stomped on it. He never would have dreamed of stomping on a half-finished American cigarette in the Soviet Union. My, how nice freedom was. He looked at the pack. Easily worth a solid trade back home. He dropped the pack onto the ground and the sexy tiger woman's grin now looked a bit depressed.

He made a decision then. He was going to go back to his room and, well, he supposed he was still going to look at internet porn as there really wasn't much for him to prepare, but regardless, he was going to take control.

No more running. No more smoking.

He was going to help fix things.

He was three steps away from the depressed tiger woman before he turned back and glanced in either direction.

No one had seen him drop it.

He picked it up and dusted it off. There was a little dirt on the tiger's cleavage, but that was all. He slid it into his pocket.

He was still in control. Smoking wasn't controlling him.

He was *choosing* to smoke.

So, half a pack and three hours into pornography, Moller knocked on his door.

Marat cursed in Ukrainian and struggled to get his pants. After pulling up his zipper, he commanded the door. *"Oh-pen."* He had an awkward shake in his voice.

Moller half glanced around his room.

Marat could feel a nervous itch as he wasn't sure if he'd closed his computer or not, but was sure that if he turned back to look, he'd only make things worse.

"Are you ready?" she asked.

Marat nodded.

"Get your shoes on and meet me at the Air Force hangar."

Fortunately, the computer was off. He hoped she hadn't noticed the pile of tissues. He pulled on his shoes and a clean, white shirt the base had provided and made his way to the hangar.

The new team was there. Five ruthless-looking bastards from America as far as Marat could tell. Moller was at the head of the team. She went over the particulars of the mission and how someone high up had given her command.

Marat spent most of the time nodding in agreement and glancing over at people who asked questions. He even narrowed his eyes as if they made a good point or had given him something to consider.

In reality, he had a very poor understanding of what was being discussed. The combination of his anxiety, Moller wearing a ponytail, his poor English skills, and his unwillingness to admit any of this made it all very difficult to understand what was going on.

He waited for everything to break before he approached Moller.

"Ehh." He tried to laugh but it came out weak. "You can tell me what we are doing?"

Moller smiled. He felt the heat and confidence all over again.

"We're going to inspect the site." She hesitated before speaking again. "And we're going to collect specimens."

1 2

THE REVOLUTION in Iran that toppled the fledgling democracy saw the ascension of the Ayatollah, a religious zealot with full control and autonomy.

Babak still remembered the videos they watched in school. The most important being when the Ayatollah had grown old and spent seven days and seven nights in endless prayer to determine who his successor would be.

It was a proud moment for all Iranians when the Ayatollah came out onto his balcony and made his announcement.

"My brothers," he said in the video. *"God has spoken to me and told me his will."*

The camera stayed focused on him, and though the crowds were massive, not a voice could be heard.

Simple silence. Complete and beautiful silence.

"God wills me to live forever."

The crowds erupted into cheers then, and though the Ayatollah's voice was amplified by speakers, he still needed to shout to be heard.

"And God has promised me that one day, I will rule the world! And he will cast our enemies into Hellfire where they will suffer for eternity for their sins against us! And we will all rule as kings!"

There would be no successor. The Ayatollah was the once and future ruler of Iran and, in some distant future, of all the world. It may be that Babak would never live to see it, but he could rest in comfort knowing he played some part in the Ayatollah's ascension as ruler of the world.

Babak's loyalty was so complete that when he was twenty, he turned his parents in to the authorities for calling the Ayatollah insane. After their execution, he was rewarded with a position in the Royal Revolutionary Guard Corps.

He trained endlessly to protect the Ayatollah with his life, and if need be, enter onto any battlefield to kill the Western bastards who plagued them.

These days, the Ayatollah made no public appearances and few pronouncements. It had been some long decades since he made the announcement upon his balcony, and he was an old man then. But proof of God's promise, he still lived and ruled Iran.

As Babak rose in rank, he was trusted with the Ayatollah's security, and he frequently saw the ruler.

The man's once-vibrant face had thinned, and his skin looked as thin as paper. Portions of his body were now replaced with cybernetics, and large, external, synthetic veins ran outside his body. Caretakers attended to him twenty-four hours a day, and his food and water were all administered through intravenous lines, which also replaced his blood twice a week.

The science wing of the Royal Revolution Guard Corps worked tirelessly to develop improvements to bring comfort to the Ayatollah, as now even speaking was painful and most of his orders had to be interpreted by his devout inner following so as not to strain the Ayatollah.

Those same devoted interpreters would sometimes spend days in prayer to pull the will of the Ayatollah from him and make it understood to others. Their burden was heavy. It became needed for them to sleep amongst the Ayatollah's harem and eat of his food to better align their spirits with the Ayatollah's and carry his will.

The Ayatollah's true age was a secret known to only a few, Babak not being one of them. He could guess that the man was well over one hundred years and possibly closing in on one hundred and fifty.

A true testament of eternal life.

But to see the Ayatollah in such a state brought misery upon Babak's soul.

"Why has he been so cursed?" Babak once asked his faith leader. *"Why will God not heal him for his great purpose? It pains me so."*

His faith leader, one of the men who interpreted the Ayatollah's will, was a broad-chested man with a thick beard. He leaned in closely to Babak and gripped him on the back of the neck. *"It is good that it pains you. Your pain brings some measure of peace to the Ayatollah. You carry some small burden for him. You must understand, we are a sinful people, and the Ayatollah carries the weight of it all. He suffers for us. We should then suffer for him."*

The thought strengthened his resolve, and all doubt was cast away.

It had been some years now since he had seen the Ayatollah, but his faith and loyalty remained unquestioned.

Babak now marched with devotion in all processions, wearing the blue CAG of his elite guard force. He carried out all missions assigned to him, both on domestic and foreign soil.

Babak was a trained killer, graduating from the finest military schools in Iran. He fought in clandestine operations, killing both Europeans and Americans. He was amongst the most hardened and experienced killers in the world.

But while he knew much about the killing of men. . .

He knew very little about demons.

Hell had opened upon Iran, and a horde of demons came screaming through.

Babak himself had fought on the front lines as the hordes of Hell expanded their relentless assault.

A massive creature, as tall as a building, walked on stalk legs. It had a ridiculous ball of a body with mouths on all sides. It plucked men and women from the ground and shoved them into either side, filling whatever mouth wasn't chewing at the moment.

It walked unabated through the streets of Tehran, and if Babak had to say, it looked more curious than hungry.

Then there were the hordes of mindless Iranian citizens who had succumbed to some plague and now fought with the enemy. They flooded the streets and devoured their brothers, all while pale, eyeless beasts leapt from rooftop to rooftop, devouring with endless hunger.

The fighting went on for days and then weeks as the Ayatollah's most loyal stood their ground for his life. But as the enemy continued, all ground was surrendered but the royal district and the palace. An array of the most powerful weapons and finest soldiers prepared to battle to the death for the Ayatollah.

Yet the palace emptied as the government began to relocate. Even the interpreters collected the royal harem to protect the Ayatollah's wives and fled on helicopters.

"Why wasn't our Supreme Leader moved with the interpreters?" Babak demanded.

"We cannot move him," the caretakers told Babak. "Any such jostling may end his life."

Babak was a man with authority and command. He called back his soldiers and told them to protect the royal palace at all costs.

The royal palace itself was a fortress with layers of underground floors and structures. They could hold back an army, if need be.

And they did.

The Royal Revolutionary Guard was a costly force, both in training and in equipment.

They proved their worth.

Babak himself fought on the lines with his men as they turned back wave after wave of endless creatures, day in and day out, using stims to forgo sleep. The palace had been preparing for an invasion by an aggressive Western force, not Hell, but their armor, weapons, and stock piles of supplies served them well.

Babak took position in a pillbox, firing his multi-barreled, heavy-caliber, locked-placement weapon so much that the ends glowed red from heat. Mindless creatures rushed toward him, and his weapon chewed them into pulp. He only ever stopped to reload.

He prayed the interpreters had fled to gather more soldiers and allies to come and rescue them, or that the Ayatollah would seize his destiny and rise up to cast these monsters back into the pit.

But until then, Babak was intent to hold.

That was, until the other horde came.

Communications came in of a secondary force moving toward Tehran, and all there assumed it must be more of the same enemy.

But Babak hadn't achieved his rank among the elite troops for loyalty alone. No, he was a keen observer to detail. Standing on the wall of the palace behind the inches of thick glass, he saw small details in the forces attacking the palace from either side. Details so small he supposed he might be imaging it.

But he didn't think so.

A different shade in skin. A different way of fighting.

A more vicious interest in killing.

Warring broods.

That much was obvious when the two first met.

They seemed to have a stronger desire for each other than they did for the people of Iran.

We're caught in the middle.

It didn't take long for that observation to settle in. It was clear as day that the large palace lay between the two hordes. The creatures flowed around the palace tearing viciously at each other.

Babak and what remained of the Royal Revolution Guard corps watched in both horror and confusion as they found themselves surrounded by some hellish war. He withdrew into the command center to better coordinate and view the fight from video.

Through it all, Babak kept the men calm and coordinated and the palace safe.

But then the walls broke.

"Sir!" a transmission came in over Babak's comm. "*The southern wall has been breached!*"

Babak froze. "How?"

Another soldier came on the line. "*They're in, they're in! They're—*"

The transmission died.

Babak made one more desperate call to his men, *"Pull back! Every-one! Into the palace! Leave the wall!"* He watched from a vid screen as his men on the outer walls raced back, firing as the horde flowed in like water through a breach.

Some of his men turned to fire. Others ran but were quickly over-whelmed.

Two men were closing in on the door, but so was the horde. There was no choice.

"Bar the door," Babak ordered with some reluctance. The main hall was shut.

Through a vid screen, he watched as his men got to the hall moments later. They beat on the door before the horde flowed onto them.

Babak looked away and picked up his rifle.

There was no one left to coordinate. He would have to go and rejoin the ranks.

That was two days ago.

Hour by hour, minute by minute, Babak fought for his life.

And practically every military man he ever knew was dead.

They fought in the hallways and made the enemy pay a heavy price for every foot they took. But while Babak's men died, the demons only seemed to multiply.

They were fought back to the royal chambers.

Babak entered the royal quarters and slammed and barred the door.

He'd left the last of his team to hold the entrance hallways for as long as they could. He could still hear their guns firing.

Babak hit the clasps on his helmet and pulled it off. It was against royal etiquette to wear it in the Ayatollah's presence.

Sweat dripped down his face as he dropped his helmet on the ground, allowing it to smack into the cold stone and roll across the floor. That too was against royal etiquette, but he was nearly to the point of collapsing. He'd been running entirely on injectable ampheta-mines for the last few days, and his heart pounded in his chest like it wanted to break out.

He couldn't remember the last time he'd slept.

Babak let his rifle fall back on its strap. He approached the red silk curtain of the Ayatollah's throne.

On a normal occasion, he would need to be announced, and even then he would not be allowed to speak directly to the supreme ruler, but these were trying times, and exceptions needed to be made.

He parted the curtain.

Years had passed since anyone beyond the closest inner circle had been allowed to see the Ayatollah. The weight of his sin was heavy upon him.

His heart dropped.

The leader of Iran and destined king of the world was a husk of a man. If not for the medical equipment that still blipped to indicate life, Babak would be certain he was dead.

His once thick, dark beard was now crisp and white. His eyes, dark red, stared at the floor. His skin had grayed beyond imagination, and countless black cables ran into his body, one leading directly into his chest.

Encased in a plastic box, an external, mechanical heart thumped inside of a gray sack of synthetic skin. It visibly beat, sending new blood into the man.

But Babak was loyal.

And he was a believer.

"Your Excellency." He fell at the feet of the Ayatollah, looking upon his gray, sandaled feet and their brown, curled and splintered toenails.

Babak had to stop and breathe. Seeing the Ayatollah in this state was more frightening than any creature.

"The enemy has breached your palace and now threatens your royal station." He fought back the pain in his voice. "Soon, they will breach your quarters, and I am all that stands to defend you. But I believe, your Excellency. I believe in your destiny and your purpose for the world. I believe you will smite our enemies and bring a golden age upon us. I beg you now to awaken and begin your great ascension. I plead with you to throw back the armies of Hell. And I—"

Babak bit off his words as the Ayatollah began to hiss. *"Ehh."* A long, dreadful gasp of air.

Babak looked up. The red, bloody eyes of the Ayatollah rested upon him. Small dots of black in the center focused on Babak.

And in that ancient gaze, though humbled with age, Babak saw the fate of the world. He rose to his feet, all doubt and fear vanquished.

He turned toward the door and drew his rifle.

There would be songs and stories of this moment, when the destiny of the world shifted and the throne was ascended. Perhaps Babak himself would have a line within it.

The gunfire beyond the door had stopped. There was now the chitter of nails on stone outside the room. He was sure he would soon die, and that was fine, but he only had one wish.

He wanted to see the Ayatollah rise from the throne and begin the first steps of his kingdom.

A MADNESS HAD SET upon the scarred Archon as he descended on Tehran. It was as if his own blood was turning into poison.

"Go," he said with human words. He pointed toward the city.

Howling with pleasure, his children set upon it while he leapt into the air with no real purpose or direction.

His wings came out, wide leather sheets of skin, and gave two powerful flaps before tightening against his back once more.

He'd yet to use his wings, but the movement came so naturally, he felt as if he'd always had them.

He went sailing through the air, breaching through a cloud and arching back down.

He smashed into a snow-covered mountain peak and rolled until he fell upon a flat ledge. The snow was cold against his bare skin, but he could endure.

What he couldn't suffer were the voices inside his head, screaming and challenging him, and making his blood flow backward.

He lost control of some limbs, one arm going weak and then the other. The Archon threw his head back and roared so loudly it echoed through the valleys.

A leg went out from under him and moved without his control. He rolled on the ground until he regained the strength in his arm. He slashed a hand into his leg and made blood pools against his nails. The pain was horrendous. He screeched again before falling off the ledge. He slid down the snow and hit another flat ledge. His body quaked and shivered. He looked up to see the mouth of a cave.

With the madness upon him, he moved into the darkness of the cave.

He stayed there, howling and jittering out insane words in a thousand different languages from beings of other worlds known to the hive mind. His mind flowed thick, and his thoughts were sharp and painful to the touch. The voices in his head formed teeth and chewed him from the inside.

Such was the pain of his existence. The misery of being a god.

The Archon crawled onto a corner and sunk his nails into his head. He dug deep enough that the pain became unbearable, but with that blinding pain he found clarity and peace.

The voices quieted, their violence ended.

The Archon sat there, nails still firmly in place. His wounded flesh throbbed. He thought of nothing but the pain.

And that brought him peace.

Days passed, until insanity loosened its grip, and the Archon could draw his fingers from his scalp. Weak from the fits, he crawled out of the cave and settled onto the ledge to look down upon Tehran.

Though exhausted, his eyes were still strong, and he could see the battle.

His children were engaging his brother's army—and they were winning.

His brother proved his weakness, for even without the scarred Archon's presence, his children were strong and his brother's weak.

A warm, golden feeling passed over him, so strange he didn't know what it was or what it meant. It was beautiful to see his children with their lust for war upon them and killing an enemy that was their equal.

Some of his children were older than he was. He fathered no brood, but his mind had passed through them and his will could bring strength or weakness upon them.

They were strong.

He was strong.

Renewed, he crouched down and then leaped into the air.

His wings unfolded and gave three massive beats to hurtle him through the air toward Tehran.

He careened into the side of a fortress and a massive puff of dust exploded into the air. Cement and stone collapsed as he got to his feet. His children were already flowing into the fortress, and they hailed his arrival with shrieks of joy. He pushed the rubble aside and walked into the fortress. The bodies and blood of men and cronux lined the hallways.

The loud clatter of firearms cracked in the distance, so he headed that way. The men were holding off his children at a tight entrance point.

The Archon sent them all a message within the hive mind.

Back.

At once, they flowed back and headed off in the other direction, intent to find different prey.

The men stopped firing their weapons for a moment, until the Archon stepped into view.

They pointed and fired.

The Archon moved with a sharp quickness unseen in this world.

Their shots blasted the hallway, smashing into the ornate stone walls. Few found the Archon, and those that did barely pierced his top layer of skin.

He was upon them before any had the chance to retreat. He whipped his claw through the first man's head, sending it hurling back. Blood sprayed from the man as the Archon turned and fanned his mouth open, sinking his teeth into the shoulder of another man and crunching through the armor.

The man screamed as the Archon tore off a bite. He spit out the first bite as it was mostly metal and took another, this time finding meat. Blood bubbled from the wound as bullets shattered against his back. He turned and hurled the injured man into the attacker, knocking him off his feet.

The Archon crouched and then leapt, smashing one man into the wall hard enough to make the stone crack and the armor crush inward. The man hissed, and his arms flailed as he fell.

Then the Archon lost interest and moved through the hallway. He grabbed the few who still remained and tore their limbs off and left them to bleed out.

A single man at the end of the hallway fired his weapon and shouted in some language the Archon had yet to learn.

The Archon fell upon him and peeled the armor sheets off as the man screamed. With the man's body exposed, he took large bites of meat.

As the Archon swallowed, he realized he was exhausted. It had been some time since he'd eaten. It was nice now, to take his time and feast.

He chewed loudly and the juice ran down his throat. He ate the entire chest of the man, and though he could eat for days, he stopped with just that.

He saw a large ornate door. Everything was silent now. He might have even left it, if not for the beauty of the door and the ferocity with which the men protected it.

He headed toward the door and passed a mirror, which caught his eye.

His pale skin was red with blood, and his eyes were completely black. His powerful wings were tight against his back, betraying their size, and still had the pink tones of being freshly grown. His tail coiled and swayed behind him like a serpent.

Though he had been healed in the fire, his spine had still been fused awkwardly from when men had thrown nuclear fires upon him. This made him slouch forward, but it did not upset him. He only observed it and nothing more.

He pushed on the door, but it was barred. With more strength, he pushed again. It cracked open.

The room was a wide hall with a red curtain that cut the room in half.

A single man in blue armor without a helmet shouted words in the same foreign language as the other men. The Archon doubted he'd ever learn it.

After he was done shouting, the man pointed a gun and fired. The Archon moved quickly while bullet casings clattered to the floor and the walls behind him exploded from the weapon's impact. The Archon jolted forward and whipped his tail at the man, piercing the man's chest with the point.

The Archon lifted the man high into the air and glared at him.

What was he doing here? What was he protecting?

The Archon had some strange interest, but it was only mild. He let the man slide off the tip of his tail and clatter to the floor, leaving the man to watch with dying eyes as the Archon approached the curtain.

He balled his fist into the fabric and tore it down.

In the space behind the curtain, some strange contraption clicked and beeped with odd cables running into a weak, crippled man.

The Archon was different from his brothers. On this world, he learned of beauty and knew there were new things to learn and experience.

But this?

He wasn't sure what this was or why it was protected so dearly.

Was it beautiful in some way? Was it important to the wounded man?

He cast a glance back. The blue-armored man was still watching.

A mild string of curiosity wove through the Archon.

But he was also pressed for time.

His tail whipped forward and smacked the ancient man's head off his shoulders. It bounced across the floor.

The Archon turned away. All of the machines stopped clicking and began a continuous buzz.

The armored man on the floor stared at the head and then at the body before giving one last gasp of breath and dying.

The Archon walked past him, no longer concerned with such strange things.

He'd wasted enough time.

He was going to meet his brother.

13

THE TRUCK'S sudden halt shook Miles awake. He groaned as he rose up and mumbled in a lazy slur. *"The fuck is. . .?"* He pulled off the hat he'd been using to block the sun.

Kevin leaned in. "Rat says we have to stop for supplies."

"Alright, alright." Miles waved Kevin back. "You smell like bad cheese, mate. We need to get you a shower pronto."

Kevin wrinkled his nose. "Not me, it's you. You've been sweating like a stuck pig back here."

Miles skewed his eyes at him and sniffed at his armpits. "Fucking hell, you're right. I smell like butter on a cow's ass. I hate the goddamn Soviet Union. I might have had to crawl through shit in North Japan and Sudan, but I never smelled like this."

"If dirty armpits aren't your thing, then you're going to be really unhappy soon. We're coming up on a few other groups of survivors. Rat eyeballed them too."

Miles yawned and stood up. "I'll deal. Just need a little legroom here is all. Did twelve hours driving and can't get more than a cat nap back here. Don't know how that Japanese bastard up there does it." He gestured toward Kevin. "Come on now, sweets. Let's pop out and stretch our legs at least."

Miles hissed as he stepped into mud. Kevin climbed down behind him with his pack on his back.

"What's this?" Miles pointed. "You don't have anything important in there, sweets. After our equipment got destroyed, even the eyeballs are trash. Afraid you'll come back and find one of these gangly bastards in here sniffing your underwear or something?"

"Why the hell are you calling me 'sweets' all of a sudden?"

"*Eh.*" Miles waved him off. "Brain's a bit foggy still, and sweets is all that came to mind."

"It's really odd that *sweets* is the first thing that came to mind." Kevin patted his bag. "If they're going for supplies, I want to make the run too.

Miles shrugged. "Suit yourself." He rounded the truck. A few of the older men in their group were talking with some of the survivors they'd found, while others were setting up fires for cooking.

Miles looked the new people over and tisked. "Not a good lady among them. No point in sticking around then. I'll head on for supplies too. Let's go see if Kota's going." Miles walked toward the side of the truck.

"Kota? You two on a first-name basis now?" Kevin asked.

"Oh yeah, mate, we're close." He held up two crossed fingers. "He's real interesting to talk with. Something that's been sorely lacking in this trip." He rolled his eyes.

"Yeah, funny. You've been a hoot too."

Miles zipped down his pants and pissed into a ditch. "*Hey.*" He glanced over his shoulder with a grin and raised eyebrows. "He even showed me his sword."

"This some kind of dick joke? If you're getting ready to flash your pecker, I'd prefer not."

"No!" Miles huffed and shook himself off. "I mean it. Bastard carries a real sword on 'em."

Kevin frowned. "Why?"

"Oh hell, I don't know, mate. So he can stab a person or two, I'd suspect."

"I know what you do with a sword, I mean why the hell would a soldier in Combat Armor Gear carry one?"

"Tell you what, you ask him yourself." Miles pointed.

Kevin turned around, startled to see Endo only a few feet away.

Endo already had his helmet on and a rifle slung over his shoulder. When he spoke, his voice came out crisply over external speakers in the armor. "Miles, you said you want to head in? I'm going for supplies now."

"Yep." Miles gave a thumbs up. "We'll be right there."

Kevin watched Endo leave before glancing back at Miles "Did he really show you his sword?"

"Nah, just fucking with you, mate. They don't carry swords."

Kevin glanced in Endo's direction then back to where Miles took a piss.

"How the hell does he pee in that?"

ENDO FOUND a speck of a town and suspected it wasn't much bigger than the dot that represented it on the map. Most Soviet towns were planned affairs, and this one looked to be more of the same. There were some half-built structures around, but for whatever reason, the Soviets seemed to have stopped years ago and moved on. It was small enough that there wasn't a rail system nearby.

Endo hoped that meant it had been spared.

A splash of blood on the ground ended that idea.

"What do you think it is?" Kevin stared at it. "It's not much blood." He looked either way. "And it doesn't seem like there's anyone else here."

"Any blood is too much, mate," Miles said. "That said, it's not enough to indicate there was a large battle."

"No," Endo agreed, "but I don't see any bodies."

They went about the town and looted what they could. Kevin stuffed a bottle of alcohol into his jacket, along with some supplies for cooking. Miles found a stock pair of sunglasses and tried them on before tossing them aside and picking up a walkie talkie from the table. He tested the battery and found it was still good. "Hey, my luck's turning around."

There wasn't much else, but they took what little food and supplies they could.

They moved as a group and finished at an office building. Endo went in, but the automated lights didn't come on. His helmet adjusted to ambient levels of light, but Miles complained behind him.

"Can't see a damn thing in here."

"Here, I found this back there." Kevin fished out a lighter and clicked it.

Endo pressed on his wrist guard, and lights illuminated from his helmet.

"Love it, mate. Got flashlights on your skull." Miles stepped in alongside him. He flashed a look back at Kevin. "Put your lighter away, fool. We don't need it so long as Kota's head glows."

Kevin snorted and put the lighter back into his pocket.

"Is it dangerous here?" Miles asked.

Kevin glanced around. "Shouldn't you have asked that before you went in?"

"Eh, too much thinking will get you killed." Miles mocked a panicked look and acted like he froze in place.

"There's something back there." Endo pointed. His helmet screen indicated movement.

"Shit." Miles winced hard and moved to get behind Endo.

"Wait here." Endo held up his rifle and walked deeper in.

There was nothing scattered on the floor or any indication of trouble. He'd been right, and it seemed to have mostly been spared.

"There someone back there?" Endo said in Russian. When no one answered, he asked again in Ukrainian. *"Is someone back there? We are not enemies."*

Endo passed by cubicles, carefully inspecting inside as he moved past and toward a counter at the end where he'd detected movement.

Nothing moved, but Endo could feel a strange stillness in the air.

Something was there.

He could sense it in his blood.

Leading with the nose of the rifle, he rounded the counter and flashed the light down.

A woman in a blue dress lay there, her hips were completely turned around backward to her chest, her body twisted up like a towel. But she was alive, and she raised her hand up to block the light from Endo's helmet.

She went to mouth words, but nothing came out.

Weak and crippled, her head swayed back and forth on her neck like some toy on a spring. Her fingers looked an inch too long, and as her head swayed back a second time, Endo noticed a third eye growing under her chin.

Endo had seen many horrible things in his life from the dead to the still-living, tortured servants of North Japan, but this. . .

She fanned her mouth open again. Endo's light caught another eye growing inside her mouth.

. . . this was the worst.

MILES'S WHOLE BODY ITCHED. The kind of itch when a person's skin tries to crawl off the body and run away. When everything pulled in the *get-the-fuck-out-of-here* direction.

It was because the woman had her mouth open, and the eye rolling inside was staring at him.

And he couldn't help but stare back.

It was set deep inside her tongue, like it must be growing out of the base of her jaw. And the worst thing of all was when she tried to blink.

Little flaps of the tongue would tighten up and shake but they couldn't quite fully blink.

Miles could only tell it was trying to blink because all of the other eyes, including the one on her chin, blinked in sync.

They tied up the damn thing or, rather, Endo did. Miles wouldn't get near the thing for all the money in the world.

Miles had stood back as Endo dove in and manhandled the thing. He lifted it and took it into the street where the light could get it. He then twisted it over and tied its arms and wrists behind its back. The whole time Miles watched in near horror.

Why the hell are you doing that? Why aren't we walking back in the other direction and burning this whole town down and going about our lives as if we never saw the hideous thing?

But he didn't say anything.

And now they were all looking at it like they paid ten cents for the freak show and wanted to get their money's worth. Worst of all, for whatever reason, the woman had decided to focus on Miles and stare into his damn eyes.

Miles felt outnumbered on account of her having four eyes and he only two.

Miles had a good minute and a half of staring at it in silence, which was an eternity when something with four eyes stared into your soul, before someone finally broke the silence.

"That thing's fucking ugly." Kevin, ever a gift for the obvious, pointed his finger at it.

It broke the spell on Miles, who stepped back before speaking, *"You think so?"* He looked at Endo. "Mate, the fuck you go and touch the thing for? Armored gloves or not, you better wash your goddamn hands." He avoided looking back at it.

"Why did this happen?" Endo asked. With Endo's faceless helmet, Miles wasn't sure if he was even looking at it.

"It's a cast off. Bad growth." Kevin tapped his head. "Corrupted chip."

Endo settled on his haunches and faced it, but Miles had his back to it. He spared a look at Endo and could see the woman and her eye reflecting off Endo's helmet. And in the reflection, she was still angled toward Miles.

He glanced back to confirm. Yep, she was still staring at him.

Miles turned away. "The hell she like me so much for?"

"Why's this bother you so much?" Kevin made a face. "We've seen a lot of nasty business so far."

"Mate, I've seen a lot of *nasty business* in my life, but never been stared at by an eyeball in a mouth. 'Sides I remember when you were crying your tits off over KGB. Why you're okay with this and so scared of that, I don't know."

"KGB will cut your dick off. This thing will just stare at you weird."

Endo leaned up. "We have to find out how to test to know it's not human."

Miles pointed his finger at its head. "Those extra eyes not good enough for you, mate? Want me to check her arsehole for a fifth?"

"No, we need it so we can test others."

"He's right, but I have a better question." Kevin tipped his head back. "Why do you think there was only one?"

Miles slowly straightened and looked back toward the trucks.

Something occurred to him.

"Only one? Bet you there wasn't."

FIVE YEARS PASSED for Erkin Kahn in the Han Chinese prison camp.

There were times when some would be permitted to leave. The guards would show up, gather the person, and walk them out.

They had served their time.

They had proven their loyalty.

Hadn't Erkin proven his?

They forgot about him, he was sure of that now.

Somewhere, someone had made a mistake on his papers and he was placed here.

For no reason.

Forgotten.

What else could there be? What had he done to deserve *this*?

What they didn't understand was that when the authorities brought him in, he was weak. Docile. He folded easily and he obeyed.

He believed.

But no, that wasn't him anymore.

They could have broken him in the beginning, but instead they hit him too hard, and to beat metal is to only make it stronger.

Erkin saw what this place really was.

They didn't want to destroy *him*; they just wanted to destroy his culture.

And that started with breaking the mind.

He would obey, but he would not break.

Perhaps that's why they held him?

Terrible days would come and go. Once the authorities had all the prisoners out in the rain, picks and shovels in hand, and digging holes. It was back-breaking work, and they did it throughout the night. And when they all had a hole dug, the guards came through to inspect.

"This one's too deep. That one is too shallow."

"This one has a crooked edge. That one's corners are too square."

"You dug them wrong. Fill the dirt in and dig it up once more."

They'd all been confused, but the guards started shouting. They all shoveled the dirt back inside.

One man collapsed, and two guards came up to him, shouting and kicking until the man stood. He collapsed a second time, and they put him in the hole.

"Fill it up," they'd ordered.

Erkin had been one of those tossing dirt.

One man cried too loudly, and they shouted at him. He kept crying.

They drew their weapons and fired.

The gunshot still rang in Erkin's ears. He'd only been a few feet away.

They dragged the body out and the man's dead eyes seemed to focus on Erkin. His fingers dragged through the soil, churning up dirt, like some part of him was afraid to move on.

But that bullet was a mercy. Why continue to live to be miserable and dig holes?

Whenever that question would come to Erkin, he would remember his wife's face and his daughter's eyes.

And he knew what he had to live for.

Somehow, Erkin was going to get out of here. Someone would eventually realize their mistake on his papers and he would be allowed out.

He knew it would happen.

He had to believe it.

He had to remain whole until then.

His wife and daughter were waiting.

He would be with them once more.

Later, someone had done the unthinkable and tried to kill a guard. Had the man succeeded, the guards might have shot everyone. Instead, they put the man in a hot box—a metal cage lined with wool and left in the sun.

The prisoners were made to toil in the sun while listening to the man's mad ravings as the heat drove him insane. The man begged and pleaded for someone to shoot him while they went about their work and education that day—picking all the stones out of a field while reciting the Chinese commandments of citizenship.

"There is not many. There is one."

"Shoot me! They're in me. On my skin they're—"

"One nation. One goal."

"Please! Someone, please!"

"Our integrity is unbreakable."

"Someone. Someone."

"We stand against our enemies, a unified people."

"Please. Please."

"For the glory of our people. For the glory of China."

"Please. . . "

"We will not fail."

"Kill. . . me. . ."

They had other ways of breaking people. Some seemed no better than systematic cruelties. Once a week, they were stripped naked, regardless of weather, and lined up for their new clothes—white shirts, white pants, and green, rubber shoes—but occasionally, for no clear reason, they would hand out an orange uniform.

That meant the prisoner had three days.

Did it mean they had not performed their duties correctly? Perhaps they had failed to impress someone?

Erkin didn't know.

He could only watch as the men who received the orange outfit went insane. One man refused to take it and ran naked from the hall. The guards arrested him, beat him, and put the outfit on him.

On the third day, the guards dragged him out to some unknown fate.

Another man took his orange outfit and then pleaded to be given a white uniform. He fell on his knees before the guards and begged, but they ignored him.

He too was gone in three days.

Each time an outfit was handed out, the inmates would become nervous and look away from whoever received it.

It was as if a disease had fallen upon them.

They were outcasts.

Plagued.

It drove the whole camp mad.

Some would blabber through the night, others would cry all day long, and a few even committed suicide by rushing the fence only to be cut down by gunfire.

But not Erkin. While the others slowly went insane, Erkin retreated into his mind.

In the calm moments between work tasks, he would sit alone in some quiet place and pull up the memories of his wife and his daughter's face. He would build a house for them within his mind.

It only worked if he did it step by step. First, he imagined going to his parents' toolshed and pulling out a shovel. It took some time to walk to the shed and then to the place where he would build the house, but within his mind he took every step and every breath. He even stopped to drink water.

And when he got to the location, he put his shovel down and dug out the first clump of dirt. He imagined huffing from the work and wiping off his sweat. It was hard work, even if it wasn't real. But it was worth it, because at times, when she'd finished work, his wife would arrive and bring him water. Not every day, but at least twice a week.

To see her meant more than anything. Her smile brought more peace than the cup of water.

But eventually he would have to open his eyes again and rejoin the real world.

It didn't matter, though. Erkin became so disciplined and strong that he began to build the house even while awake. He became a man of two minds, one that could dig and recite Han Chinese doctrine, and another, deeper within his soul, that built his house.

It took weeks to finish the foundation, as he did it all alone, but when it was done, he gathered bricks and mixed cement, bringing it all step by step. It was hard work beneath the sun, but his soul healed every time his wife stopped by with the water.

Sometimes, she would bring his daughter.

She should have been at school during that time, but in this world, there was no mandated education, and his daughter was allowed to visit.

It brought a tear to Erkin's eye to see how much she'd grown and changed since he'd last seen her in the real world. Thankfully, she had her mother's eyes and looks and not Erkin's dull face.

With the walls up, they had to put up a plastic sheet to act like a roof. That was useful as the rainy season was coming.

Within the real world, Erkin was made to crack rocks with a hammer and sing the Han Chinese national anthem. He sang every note with a smile on his face. He even heard the whispers from the others that he'd finally broken.

But no.

No. No. No.

He hadn't broken.

The rain had just come, and he was forced to take a day off.

It was good that they had the plastic up. The rain had come suddenly as his wife was on her way over. Her hair was soaked along with his daughter's dress.

They all laughed and cuddled now beneath the plastic tarps inside the house he'd built. He couldn't work today, not in this weather, but that was all well and good. He'd been so focused that he really hadn't had much time for his family. And now he got to sit with them and talk and tell his daughter stories as they waited for the rain to end.

"Do you see that land over there?" he asked her. *"Your grandfather and grandmother played there."*

She wrinkled her nose and grinned as she tried to imagine it.

Smiling, he tapped her nose and pointed again. *"One day, you will be a mother, and I a grandfather, and I'll watch my grandchildren play in that field."*

The storm passed in time, far shorter than it may have in the real world, but that was fine. They came out and saw the sun in the distance. Erkin squeezed his wife's hand and cupped his daughter's shoulder.

He knew then that in time, their storm would pass, and in time he would be with his wife and daughter.

And all would be worth it.

He woke up the next morning, intent to begin on the roof. They lined up for laundry, and Erkin stripped bare like everyone else.

Inside his mind, he pulled the plastic down on a portion of the roof and wheeled over the materials.

It was difficult as the sun was particularly hot today, but he would be fine so long as his wife brought him water. All would be—

"Here." The officer in charge of laundry pulled Erkin from his thoughts and set an orange suit on the counter.

Erkin stared at it. If his mind were glass, then it had begun to crack.

He looked up at the officer in charge of laundry, not angry but confused. "But I didn't finish the house?"

"Move." The man pointed. "Next."

"I didn't finish the house," Erkin reiterated.

"Shut the fuck up. Move out of the line." The guard pointed again.

Inside Erkin's mind, the ground shifted. The house collapsed.

It was dark there, and he remembered crying. What had he done wrong? Had he built on a bad foundation? Had the rain gotten in somehow and weakened things? Hadn't he been careful this entire time?

What had he done wrong?

His mind was so focused on the house that when he finally came to in the real world, he was screaming and the guards were beating him. A few feet away, the officer with the laundry had his hands on his face. Blood poured between his fingers. Erkin had one of his eyes clutched in his hand.

"I didn't finish the house!"

Erkin raved even as they beat him. Something cracked against his ribs, and clubs slammed against his back. But he was a man of two minds, and while one was being beaten, the other was standing at the foot of his collapsed house. . .

"I didn't finish!"

. . . and wondering where his wife and child were.

It was hard to be sure what happened next. Erkin had a vague understanding of them putting the orange suit on him. He also remembered several other beatings through the next couple of days, but if that was because he raged, pleaded, or simply refused to work, he didn't know.

On the last day, men came and took him. He expected then that he would be shot, but instead he was dragged into a building and tossed inside a cell.

It was cool in the cell. The sun didn't blister his skin here.

Did they think this was a punishment?

He got onto his knees and entered the dark hollows of his mind.

Inside, he picked up a jack hammer and smashed apart the remaining walls of his house. He pushed the rubble aside and brought over a new wheelbarrow full of materials, intent to start over once more. This time, he'd do things right.

But the tire on the wheelbarrow was flat. He had to shove it through the dirt like a plow, straining with each push. That in itself may not have worked in the real world, but here he forced it.

Next, when he got to the foundation, he reached for a brick. It melted in his hand.

His eyes flared open. The world was turning on him.

He threw the slop aside and grabbed another brick. It too melted.

Screaming, Erkin grabbed another with both hands and held it in place. He squeezed them into shape and planted them in place.

The sun grew hotter then. Blisters formed on his back near instantly, but it didn't matter. He could take the pain.

He was there for days, rebuilding the walls and structure, even as the sun blasted him and the rain pelted him.

His wife didn't come, not once, but he was sure that was because she didn't want to bother him. He would finish the house and then go to find her.

He got all the walls up in half the time it took before, but as he stood back to watch, they bent in the middle like soft clay and collapsed.

And there was laughter. From all places and all corners of his mind.

"Get up." Someone in the real world lifted Erkin. Had he been here for days or only hours? He didn't know. He couldn't remember eating or sleeping.

Half aware of what was happening, he was led into a truck. All the while, his mind kept laughing at him.

They drove, but Erkin faded deeper into his mind again. Through the echoes of laughter, he took the jack hammer once more and knocked the walls down.

He would build the house once more, even if he had to build a kiln and produce every brick on his own, or swill his blood into the cement in exchange for water.

He would build the house, and he would have his family back once more.

Nothing would stop him.

Hands within the real world grabbed Erkin and dragged him out of the truck. He stumbled along, neither resistant nor compliant, and only partially aware.

Several men in military uniforms put him on a gurney and took straps across his body, buckling him into place so he couldn't move at all. They tightened a gag over his mouth.

He was pushed down a hallway, and though there were bright lights overhead, he didn't close his eyes each time they blinded him.

They pushed him into a large gymnasium, and Erkin heard the laughter grow louder.

He began to pull from his mind as he realized the laughter was in this world and not the other. But no, it wasn't laughter. It was screams.

And gunshots.

Focusing now on the present, Erkin twisted his head. He was in a massive room full of hard, glass walls, doctors, and people strapped to gurneys.

People screamed as soldiers patrolled around, occasionally firing a round or blasting fire at something.

Erkin twisted his head in the other direction. Blood sprayed up on the glass, and a doctor screamed and thrashed about. A soldier stepped inside and blasted the room with fire, melting the man.

The soldiers with Erkin pushed him toward the glass walls and into a room. Amidst the backdrop of screams, Erkin jerked his head back and forth trying to figure out what was going on. A doctor approached him with a scalpel. It was only then that Erkin began to moan against his gag.

The doctor had sweat rolling down his face and tired eyes like he'd been working too hard. He took the blade and pressed it into Erkin's arm.

The beatings had been numb and Erkin had barely felt them, but for whatever reason, he felt every bit of the blade. Screaming against the gag, he twisted to watch the doctor slit open his bicep and display the muscle beneath it. Erkin thrashed about as the doctor grabbed a metallic canister in one hand and a syringe in the other. He twisted the top of the canister, and a cool mist rolled out. Moments later, a long, clear wisp spooled out of the tube and reached toward Erkin. It slid in between the fibers of his muscle tissue, and new pain surged up Erkin's arm.

The wisps tightened, and a fat, pink nub pulled up to the top of the canister. More wisps came out, and it dug into Erkin's wound. They slid between his veins and muscle tissue, then the creature practically jumped from the canister and into his arm.

Erkin felt it sliding around beneath his skin and gliding up toward his heart.

He heaved against the gag as he felt the wisps tighten around his spine.

Electrical shocks pulsed through his system making his head jerk with shock. Erkin looked toward the doctor, but he was standing patiently, his syringe in hand.

Erkin moaned. He felt the wisp snake toward his brain. He shivered violently as they dug into his soft tissue.

Black clouds of thought and immersion rolled over his being.

Somehow a single word popped into his brain. It was his wife's name.

With his mind flashing and burning, he tried to say her name over the gag, but wasn't able to.

A dark being, hiding within gray shadows, lifted into the air on massive legs. She was immense and powerful, and her very presence choked Erkin's soul.

He was pulled into a new world.

He felt his consciousness push out of his body, but he dug his fingers in. And though it was hard to think, even as he tried to moan his wife's name, Erkin struggled.

I will be with my wife.

I will hold my daughter again.

I will build my family a house.

He pushed back against the shadows and the presence. As their thoughts sought to smother his life, he screamed in defiance.

If he was in a new world, and if this being truly existed, Erkin stood up and bellowed curses. It—she—wanted his submission.

But he would not bow to her.

He would never bow again to anything.

With vague awareness of the real world, Erkin felt the doctor come close and put something into his arm.

The darkness began to recede, but Erkin struggled to breath while his eyes rolled into his head. His heart had been thumping, but it slowed. Each pump shook his whole body.

"He's dying," the doctor said. The voice echoed in Erkin's mind. "His heart's stopping."

Erkin's entire body went limp. He gave it all up.

There would be no house.

He heard one last word from the doctor before the darkness came. *"Dead."*

Zhao watched from a one-way mirror up high. This was the largest gymnasium they had, and they clustered all of the volunteers in one place.

Things had been cleaner before when they were using dedicated and loyal soldiers of the Chinese empire, each picked for their unmatched loyalty and service.

The tests all failed, and China needed all of its soldiers.

But they still had many prisoners.

Despite all the information they'd stolen from the Americans, not one of their tests had succeeded. All the soldiers had either changed or died.

Wu, Zhao's spymaster, recommended a new strategy.

"Perhaps we should prefer quantity over quality."

Zhao watched now as a hundred operations were going on at once. All within the same facility as flame soldiers patrolled and prevented any breakout.

The room was filled with screams, blood, and loyal subjects. The doctors were taking precise notes on the change so that when they finally succeeded with one of these deviants, they could apply that knowledge to more trusted individuals.

But these too all failed.

Zhao had better things to do than witness countless failures.

With a wave of his hand, he showed his irritation. "Dispose of the bodies. Continue operations. Contact me if there are any changes."

Mr. Wu bowed his head and said nothing as Zhao left.

Erkin woke up gasping for breath. Something was wrong with his eyes. He couldn't see anything. Hands held him down.

Was this Hell? Was he dead?

He struggled, and the hands moved. They weren't gripping, but only pressing on him. As he pushed to get room, water dripped on his face. He wiped it away.

It might be Hell. He wasn't sure, but it was hard to move. He was so weak, and he couldn't remember the last time he ate or drank anything.

He tried to scream but his throat ached. It only came out as a low moan. He felt the wound on his bicep open up as he struggled. The pain made him hiss.

With a spark of life, a pilot flame came on in the corner of the ceiling, illuminating the room.

Erkin was piled with dead bodies.

Gasping, Erkin pulled his head up. The dead were all around him. It hadn't been water that leaked on him but blood from a corpse.

With panic racing across his body, he looked back up to the pilot flame. There was a nozzle just below it. Erkin knew that soon a flammable gel would shoot through the nozzle and burn everything in the room.

He'd done work in a place like this before.

It was an incinerator.

"*Help*," he whined, his voice still weak.

Nothing happened.

The other pilot lights lining the ceiling came on.

Erkin took a deep breath and screamed so loudly he thought his throat would burst.

"*Help!*"

Seconds later, high up in the air, a door opened and a beam of light came in. Someone stuck their head through and then leaned back out to yell.

Erkin's throat throbbed and while staring up at the open hole he had to focus to stay awake.

I will be with my wife.

I will hold my daughter again.

I will build my family a house.

Zhao arrived in his office a short time ago and was preparing for a meeting with his generals when his secretary entered the room. She bowed her head and waited to be addressed.

"Yes?" Zhao said.

She raised her head, but kept her gaze low, not making eye contact. "A message has arrived from Mr. Wu. He says they have succeeded and now have a man in custody."

Zhao puffed up his chest, finally he had good news.

"Excellent. Tell Mr. Wu I will be arriving for inspections tomorrow."

The woman nodded her head, "Yes, Mr. Chairman." She bowed deeper and backed away, preparing to leave.

"One more thing." Zhao said. "Instruct Mr. Wu to amplify Operation Dragonskin."

15

Warsaw was the launch point to take back all of the Soviet Union. It had the best airfields and a holdout civilian population still fighting.

It was a jewel.

"Warsaw will put us in striking range of other high-priority targets. Take it back and we can cut the horde apart," Garin had told his officers back in Berlin. *"But it's big and Alice can't take it alone. We're moving in with full force."*

Alice didn't care. She watched the tanks and trucks line up to head out as she put on her helmet. Infantry men saw her walking amongst them and hailed her.

"The Red Bitch of Berlin!"

There was excitement in the air. The kind of thrill when the enemy pushes your back against the wall and you begin to push back. Garin held up the trust of the men. He too was a patriot with battlefield wounds and a competent commander.

But with Alice in their ranks, the soldiers were fearless.

Alice returned to the officers command center as the ground troops headed off. She would follow them shortly in a dropship.

Garin greeted her as she entered. He took a moment to rub his synthetic jaw, the black skin weave tugging where it had bonded to his flesh.

Alice imagined it was painful. She remembered how it felt when they bonded her arm together.

Garin revealed nothing more than an annoying itch.

As Alice walked over to look at the vid screens and watched the troops speeding toward Warsaw, Garin came up next to her. When he spoke, his voice came out rough, a symptom of the new jaw.

"At this rate, we'll soon be prepared to retake Moscow."

Alice said nothing, only nodded.

"Can we count on you to stay with us for the duration?"

"Yes." She still didn't look away from the screens.

There was a pause before Garin spoke again. "Why do you stay with us?"

Alice shifted her gaze toward the general.

"I want to kill them. All of them."

Garin stared back at her, as if he were trying to understand.

No one possibly could.

He nodded his head and spoke once more.

"We'll see that you do."

THE BATTLE HAD ALREADY BEGUN when Alice's ship went speeding overhead. She looked out the window to see lines forming and creatures flowing out from the city centers.

The red light in the center of the dropship flashed, and it matched the calm, dull beat of Alice's heart.

Thump-thump.

The cage doors opened, and the ship cables disconnected. With a smooth, metal whine, she dropped into the air, but her heart remained the same.

Thump-thump.

Calm. Determined. Ready.

The pilot, an expert dropship captain, aimed for the city center, and Alice slammed down right into the melee.

The cage doors opened, and she stepped out. The world slowed as soldiers ran past her, their rifles firing. She could hear the *clank-clank-clank* of a tank somewhere at her side as a mass of cronux flooded through the streets and came climbing across the buildings, defiant of gravity.

This was the largest force she'd ever deployed against. She felt a great weight in the hive mind, like a sheet pulled tight and a bowling ball placed in the center, everything rolled in that direction—a void that swallowed all.

Alice resisted.

With soldiers running past her and firing, she held her hands out to her side and closed her eyes. She needed control. If she lost herself, her brain could scramble.

Standing still, with her team forming up on her sides, she took two deep breaths and drank the battle.

When she opened her eyes, her mind was a blade, sharp and in hand.

She turned off her external sound and had silence within her armor, except for her gentle breathing and the quiet whine of the CAG gears.

There was a flash as a tank fired, and its shell hit a building where a mass of cronux clung. The building collapsed in a puff of fire and dust. Alice heard none of it in the silence of her armor.

Alice took another breath.

In.

And out.

A wave of once-men came screaming through the dust, and Alice held up her hand and in her grip she held their lives.

She crushed her fingers, and the first wave collapsed. She waved her other hand aside, and the second wave fell upon the first. Puffs of flame and rifle fire shot out across the line, sending black clouds and bullet casings onto the battlefield.

Alice walked amongst them, the screen inside her helmet shifting and adapting to the smoke and dust. Though she could not see far in front of her, she continued patient steps with her team at her side.

The dust cleared. Alice saw a gunship helicopter strafing a line. A fat cronux with staunch legs knelt down and leapt into the air. It hit the helicopter and made it spin out of control until it smashed into a building, sending up a new wave of smoke.

Another gunship came by, and Alice saw a second cronux prepare to leap.

She reached for it and felt into its mind.

A dull thing with complicated mechanics within its brain that it used to propel itself.

Alice thrusted her will upon it and squeezed. The creature burst, spraying acid at the cronux near it, and melting them into the ground.

One of Alice's team smacked her on the arm, and when she glanced over, he pointed in the air.

A flock of birds were tearing apart a rooftop rifle squad. A flame trooper shot fire at it, but they picked at his back. He burst open with an intense flame. The flame trooper fell off the edge and smashed into the ground while the birds went for the others.

Alice reached her hand toward the birds and waved away.

The birds dive bombed toward the ground and peppered the streets with their bloody bodies.

Alice took another calm breath within the silence of her armor. Her mind stretched further as she felt the full weight of the horde within the city.

Her thoughts grew thin, and the void pulled her toward the darkness, even as she clung to her reality.

But Alice took another breath and filled her lungs.

She exhaled and took another breath.

She was still human.

But even with as much power as she had, there were too many enemies, and decisions had to be made.

She felt a pull within the hive mind to a large apartment building. The cronux had nested there and were picking it apart room by room.

Some were pouring out and threatened to attack the flank of the piercing army.

But there were people there. Some of them were hanging out the windows right now and screaming to the approaching soldiers.

Alice pointed to the building and spoke with a smooth voice.

"Take it."

A soldier nodded, as their comm was still linked to hers. He glanced at the building and must have been giving commands, though Alice couldn't hear it.

Seconds later, artillery shells came down from the sky and smashed into the walls, turning it into a burning inferno and killing all within.

People and cronux alike.

Alice watched it for one moment and then looked away.

The fight wasn't over.

So was the way of war.

THE BATTLE DIDN'T TAKE LONG. The horde collapsed, and the soldiers mopped up the stragglers with very few military casualties.

Civilian casualties were unspecified.

Alice pulled her helmet off and held it at her side as she watched Soviet troops marching through the street. The surviving civilians were ordered to remain in doors, but they hung from the windows and cheered the troops.

One of Alice's team members came up alongside her and pushed the clasp on his helmet. It puffed and rose up, and he pulled it off.

It was Novikov, a man with a thick jawline and blonde hair—squad captain of the team.

"Congratulations, Ms. Winters," he said in accented English. "You've achieved something great."

Alice looked up at him. This was the first time anyone on her team had tried to speak with her on anything that wasn't mission related.

She said nothing, only nodded.

"Why is it you look so sullen?" he asked. "With Warsaw in hand, we will be back in Moscow in no time. This is a new dawn for the world and our countries."

"I don't like it." Alice shook her head. "It was too easy."

"Easy?" Novikov asked. "Successful, yes, but easy?" He frowned.

Alice turned her eyes back on him once more.

"Easy."

THE JANISSARY HAD ways and means that others did not. He knew how to grab the fabrics of the hive mind and pull the sheets around him.

To hide within the darkness.

Alice Winters couldn't find him.

But he could find her.

Oh yes, Alice Winters was loud and boisterous. Each move she made shot thunder through the world and beat a drum.

Such was the way of warriors like her.

Loud and slow of thought.

When the Janissary moved, he did so with quiet steps that were easily missed, a shadow within a shadow.

As Alice Winters went about with her thirst for blood, killing the Janissary's troops, he was building a fence and guiding her down a path.

He would wait for her mind to fill.

Then he would step from the shadows.

With Alice Winters thundering and drumming in the distance, the Janissary sat amongst his dark acolytes, and together they gathered the void.

The void was not a place.

The void was a tool.

Together, with his dark acolytes, they strung their hands together and reached down into the dwellings of the void and dipped their fingers into the red strands of the chimera.

They pulled them back.

A thousand minds and more connected once more to the Janissary and his dark acolytes as they sat in humble silence, weaving their minds together.

The Janissary pulled the strands taut and whispered a single word. The voices of each of his acolytes echoed in kind.

Now.

THE THING that wore Niklas Koch's face had gone into Germany as a refugee, and though he did not have a full understanding of what was going on, his brain could calculate responses better than previous generations of chimera.

"What's your name?" some person asked him.

"Niklas Koch. I am a laborer," he said without making eye contact.

"Where are you from?"

"Germany."

"No, what city?"

That part didn't click, and Koch's mind rolled.

"Germany," he said once more.

"Are you feeling all right, friend?"

"I am from Germany."

The man patted him on the shoulder. "Get some food."

The thing that wore Niklas Koch's face entered a soup kitchen and got in line when he felt a stiff pull reconnecting him within the hive mind.

And then a command.

Now.

He turned toward a table behind him. Lines of men and women were there, each quietly eating their soup.

The thing that wore Niklas Koch's face fanned his mouth open as wide as his shoulders and revealed all three sets of teeth.

ON ONE OF the earliest days of *Gray's* life, he'd stepped aboard a train within the Soviet Union. The train had a living floor that was soft and screamed as he stepped upon it, but Gray didn't mind, he didn't mind much of anything. He only held the railing as the train sped down.

Where it was going, or when it would get there were not concerns. Gray had few concerns at all.

Gray was more dull than his brothers, and had only a vague impression of his own existence. What he did and how he did it were more due to reaction and instinct than purpose and control.

At some point he'd gotten off the train, and moved between groups of people as they went up and down mountains, across lands, and through rivers—small refugee groups fleeing the devastation.

Someone asked him a question at one point and he didn't know how to answer, so he remained silent.

"We'll call you Gray," the person said.

Why they did this, or what that name meant, he didn't know.

But within his group they crossed territories and went deeper in land.

There was a strong instinct in Gray to go farther and farther, to touch lands his brothers had yet to tread on.

Italy.

He heard the others say it with some pride, but he only remained silent.

When they arrived at a fenced border. Men with guns made them line up. Gray felt a sudden tug, and his knees went weak.

After that moment of shock as he reconnected to the hive mind, there was a voice within the darkness.

Now.

Gray twisted his head. The cartilage in his neck snapped and cracked as muscle fibers unfolded beneath his skin. An armed guard walked down the line, talking to each of the migrants.

When he got close to Gray, he said something, but Gray didn't hear him.

Gray's fingers were stretching with violent cracking and his neck extended into the air.

The guard said something in confusion and took a step back.

Gray's head, now on a neck several feet long, thrust down and bit the guard on the neck. Blood sprayed everywhere as people started screaming.

Gray pulled his head back, and his mouth flayed open.

He found a greater focus now.

This was more fun than traveling.

16

WHEN MOLLER DECIDED to go back in, she contacted Roles and told him that Marat was sure the gate was still up and requested approval to re-enter the Soviet Union covertly.

"If that gate is active, top priority is bringing it down, but we're doing it without Soviet aid. They think it's destroyed, so you have the chance to secure their files and collect samples of the parasites. I'll send you a team. Men we can trust to keep their mouths shut. My sources say they've located a decommissioned manual railcar in the station just outside Krasnodar, but you'll have to get it repaired. Krasnodar is under siege but the rail station is outside the city limits, so you shouldn't have any trouble. Wear Soviet CAG. We're walking a tightrope with the Soviets. Anything could set them off. Don't get caught."

Secure their files? That's what Roles wanted. Whatever information they had inside the bunker.

It seemed that even with the Soviets' foot on death's door, the great game of empires continued.

It didn't matter. She would do what she was ordered to do.

"Confirmed."

She spent the next few days arranging things when the team came over—five CIA operatives, all with military experience. Roles had sent gear too, plastic fitted cases with no markings.

Moller got the team together and opened up the cases.

Soviet CAG.

This was a black operation.

The team got suited up but Marat hadn't received the training for it. The best she could do was a radiation suit that wouldn't look out of place in the Soviet Union.

He came out of the equipment room with the suit fully on—simple gray protective gear that wouldn't do much at all in a fight.

She knew that because she had one just like it on Mars when everyone else was in CAG.

The team loaded into a black wing helicopter, just like the one that had picked them up out of the Soviet Union. It could fly under any radar and if they were careful, not risk the automated surface-to-air missile batteries.

The black wing took off and Moller, already in CAG, had her seat next to Marat.

He had his helmet off and busily tapped his fingers against his legs.

Moller tapped his shoulder and pointed to his helmet and then his head. Their internal comms system was the only way to hear anything over the rotor blades.

Marat nodded and slid it on. Though her helmet entirely hid her face, she could see his through a plastic screen.

"You alright?" she asked.

Marat nodded, and grinned. "I only need cigarette."

"You have synthetic lungs now Marat, you have to give them up. They can kill you."

He gave a weak nod and glanced out the window as they passed into Soviet airspace and saw the beginning of land.

He pointed and spoke with the clearest English she'd heard from him.

"So could anything down there."

THE SUN HAD ALREADY SET over the Soviet Union as the helicopter came to hover not far above a beach. Those in CAG jumped out and landed on the beach with little impact.

Marat had to toss a rope out and slide down it.

He'd gone fine for a second or two, but he'd over estimated his upper body strength.

He ended up letting go and falling into the shallow water of the beach.

"*Shit,*" he hissed in Ukrainian as he leaned up from the water. If the suit wasn't airproof, he'd had soggy underwear as the waves lapped up near him.

A small light flashed twice from the helicopter, and Moller looked up to it. She pressed a button on her wrist guard, and a soft red light flashed three times on her helmet.

The helicopter flashed once more and flew off.

"Come on," Moller said as she stepped into the water and offered Marat her hand. "We've got some ways to go."

While Marat was busily wiping the sand off his ass, the other operatives were already out securing a vehicle to get their team to the Krasnodar rail center.

Marat walked up with Moller onto the beach, and the team had already secured two cars in less time than it had taken for Marat to wipe the sand off his ass.

They piled in and began the drive there. Marat wished they could have just taken the helicopter all the way into Krasnodar, but it was too risky and only about a two-and-a-half-hour drive there.

But that was two and a half hours of Marat sitting in the back and twiddling his thumbs, wishing he had a cigarette if only because he had nothing else better to do.

After some time they pulled into the maintenance station. It was a bit outside of the city, where they could easily work on the train cars without the heavy traffic of urban life.

They pulled up and one of the CIA drivers spoke. "Looks like this place wasn't bothered."

"Why would it be?" another operative said. "No one lives here, they just come out this way for work. Might be squatters though looking to ride out the chaos. Better keep the rifles ready." He gripped his weapon with both hands.

It didn't go unnoticed by Marat. He didn't particularly like the idea of shooting people trying to *ride out the chaos*, but then again, he wasn't the one carrying a gun, so he wasn't allowed to decide who they shot.

The cars all stopped and they piled out.

Marat stepped out too and felt his knees crack. He groaned and stretched.

Moller pointed at Marat. "You just stay here while we clear the place." She glanced over at one of the men. "You keep him safe."

The man nodded while the team moved off into the station.

When they were alone, Marat glanced over at the man as he took a seat on the hood of one of the cars. He rested his rifle on his leg.

"You, cigarette?" Marat said, gesturing as if to smoke.

The man stared at him for a moment. His CAG betrayed no thought or emotion. *"You asking me if I want one or if I have one?"*

"You have. Give me one please." Marat tried to grin but it felt wet and fake.

"I don't smoke, buddy." He raised his hands.

Marat nodded and took a few steps away. The Krasnodar loomed in the distance. Marat had never been there personally, but he'd heard its reputation.

Both beautiful and wealthy, it was the capital of its administrative division within the Soviet Union, and only an hour or two on the bullet train to Moscow.

But now, Marat could see fires consuming some of its large buildings and the flash of weapon fire.

They were under siege.

Marat watched for a moment and wondered how many people were there just like him. It was hard to imagine that the horror there had come out of the gate he helped build. That mistake was a terrifying thing, but it had been *so small* compared to all this.

Seeing it here, live and in real life, Marat had the sinking feeling.

He had a hand to play in the end of the world.

Marat heard the military people call it a siege because there was no active fighting. Only survivors running and hiding while monsters hunted them.

But again, he thought of how this all came out of one little gate and got so big.

How much bigger could it get?

The whole world.

There was that. A few more mistakes in hand, and this would be all around the world.

He was left to sit and stare at the city for the time it took them to secure the train.

A voice buzzed over their internal systems. *"Train is secured and repaired. Please come in."*

"You hear that?" the CIA operative said as he leaned off the car. "You ready?"

Marat gave one last look at Krasnodar and imagined he could hear the screams in his ears. "I'm ready."

———

MOLLER FOUND THE TRAIN CAR. It was a single service engine, used to travel the rails and make repairs. It wasn't a full passenger car, but it was more than capable of transporting her small team.

One of the operatives had to crawl inside the engine cavity and work some magic to get it going, but it wasn't long before they got it in and started off.

The train wasn't nearly as fast as the bullet train that could have gotten them to Moscow in two hours or so, but it was still considerably faster than a car. They expected to be in Moscow in a few hours.

The operatives were all staring out the window as they passed. Moller couldn't blame them. It wasn't everyday you got to go this deep into the Soviet Union, or have the chance of spotting some alien creature.

But Marat by contrast was slouched over and staring at the floor.

He didn't want to see what was happening.

Moller decided to leave him alone.

The train hadn't been going for more than an hour when one of the CIA officers from the operator's booth spoke over their channel.

"Moller, I see lights up ahead."

"Helmets on, heads down," Moller said as she grabbed her helmet and set it on her head. It sank down and hissed when it sealed. All the others did the same. "Cut the car lights," she ordered the woman in the operator's booth.

A second later, the lights all went off in the car and her helmet adjusted to the ambient light a second later.

"What is it?" one of the men said behind her, crouching down behind a bench.

"They have control of the rail system, there's no telling what it is," Moller answered, and kept low, but at the right angle to see what was coming.

On the other side of the tracks, a train came speeding their way with the front lights on.

"Don't let them see you," Moller ordered and tucked her head low. "They might think we're just an automated car."

Moller adjusted the dial on her helmet settings. It zoomed in on the car.

It was a horror show.

"My God," she whispered.

A strange pink and purple substance like veins and flesh had grown over the car. Flaps and lumps of misaligned growth spread across it with massive, dark tumors growing in the center of patches of veins. The tumors pulsed as if they were a beating heart, and Moller could see things that looked like failed attempts at eyes or hands hanging on the train. One large eye was on a tumor, but it was spinning around without focus.

"What in the fuck is that?" one of the operatives said.

"I don't know, but it's moving a hell of a lot faster than we are, everyone get your heads down." Moller ordered again.

"Let's hit it with an RPG and blow it to hell," one man said.

"Negative. Don't draw attention."

They all ducked their heads, and Moller pressed her back to the bench. She had her rifle up, tight and ready.

The rails rattled as the oncoming car closed in. There was a quiet whine.

Moller tensed. It grew louder as it closed in.

The train lights illuminated inside their car as it sped by. The whine became intensely loud. The processors inside Moller's helmet evened out the sound to prevent it from being damaging, but when she glanced over at Marat, he had his teeth clenched together and his hands pressed to his ears. His suit wasn't meant for this kind of stress.

The rail rattled violently as the car passed. The screaming continued. It wasn't one solid voice but many, like creatures had melted into the train and it hurt to be part of it.

Lights from the other train car flashed in and out of Moller's car, painting odd shadows of creatures moving within, but it sped by so quickly she couldn't make out anything clearly

The car passed and the flashing light stopped. Moller peeked over the edge to see the train speeding away. Some strange, fleshy growth was in the back window jolting back and forth like it was channeling electricity as it sped away.

"There you go," Moller said to her team. "That's your first encounter."

THEY RODE the train until they got a few miles outside of Moscow and pulled it into a service lane.

Moller herself opened the hatch on the roof and climbed out on the top. She looked either way down the tracks and saw nothing. There was certainly no guarantee that a speeding car might not come down this way.

The rails leading into Moscow were high and sailed between buildings. They were already a hundred meters in the air. Moller peeked over the edge too—lots of trees and nothing else. She supposed Soviet designers had wanted to beautify the area around Moscow and had planted trees near the rails.

Half the city was starving, but at least it wasn't an eye sore.

One by one the others followed behind onto the tracks and then to a metal grating walkway used by workers just off to the side of the rails.

They found a ladder that took them down one of the large pillars and were able to hit the ground. From there they worked out their map and took the long path toward the black site.

"This whole area is infested, but the horde has moved, so be careful." Moller told them.

They kept their rifles ready and stayed along the path.

But as they got closer to the location, their internal comms began to fuzz out.

"*Moller I—having—the—*" one operative said and tapped her helmet.

"Anyone else having trouble?" Moller put the command across channels and saw the people shrug and shake their heads. They couldn't understand her.

Moller twisted a dial on her gauntlet and opened up her exterior speakers, she adjusted the volume to keep it low.

"Switch to exterior sound. Our communications channel has failed," her voice emitted from speakers on her helmet.

The others nodded and did the same.

"What happened?" a man with a rifle tucked up in his arm asked.

"This happened on Felicity too. When the gate was up, it interfered with our communications. I don't know why." Moller shook her head. "Be careful, though, as anything can hear us now."

After sometime they got to an overlook where they could see the base.

"There it is." Moller pointed. Marat came up alongside her and nodded.

Most of the area remained, even the fencing around the bunker, but there were piles of dead, along with several large vehicles and towers set up.

It looked like the Soviet Army had already come in and failed to contain the threat.

"They must have used a Phantom class nuke," one of the operatives said. "It fried their nervous systems, but it didn't destroy the area."

"What about the Soviets? They nuked them too?" someone asked.

"Negative. They were already dead." Another operative pointed. "You can see the blood."

Moller got down on one knee and adjusted her dial again, her vision zoomed onto the spot. There were patches of blood on the vehicles, along with dead soldiers on the ground. Some were in CAG and missing limbs, others were officer class in bare uniforms.

Moller's helmet screen flashed yellow and painted a shape on a patch of land.

Movement detected.

One of the soldiers had a parasite. He moved awkwardly, apparently crippled by whatever happened. He dragged across the ground.

The closer Moller looked, the more she saw.

The dead men writhed, but with slow, agonized movements that were easy to miss.

One operative adjusted the dial on his gauntlet to barely above a whisper. *The Phantom really fucked them up.*

Moller nodded.

Another flash of yellow and the docking bay lift doors on the bunker shook and opened. They were large, reinforced metal doors big enough to drive a truck through.

When they fully opened there was a shadow behind them.

Something stepped out of it.

A large, two-legged beast that hunched over. Unlike most cronux, it had eyes, but they were maligned, one much bigger than the other in its misshapen head.

It took two steps out of the lift and looked around.

Moller's heart crawled into her throat as she swore its gaze passed over their position, but if it saw them, it didn't react.

There was more movement in the shadows of the lift, and people walked out alongside the cronux.

"Are those…" someone trailed off.

People?

Moller shook her head. "No, it can't be."

The beast watched as the people walked away from it without so much as a second glance back.

The people started on the dirt trail road leading up to the bunker and headed off.

"What do we do now?" an operative asked.

Moller let out a breath. "We get inside and figure out what the hell is going on."

"What about that big ugly thing?" the operative asked.

Moller glared at the creature as it turned around to re-enter the bunker, swinging its large tail.

"We kill it."

17

THE PEACE ACCORDS, a hard-fought truce to the bloody conflict in South America, had collapsed with the discovery of new mineral deposits.

It seemed that Venezuela no longer felt the need to honor past agreements now that it was going to collect wealth from the largest lithium vein on the planet.

John just got off a call with the US ambassador in Venezuela. *"I've tried talking to President Leon. He won't budge. He's said that the American peacekeepers are to leave his country within seventy-two hours, or he'll have them arrested. He will be signing legislation to formally end discussions on the peace accords later this afternoon. He's going to broadcast it on TV."*

Venezuela, Peru, Columbia, Brazil, and every other nation in South America were in a three way war with the countries forming alliances that changed so often, John didn't know which side any one of them belonged to anymore.

"Venezuela is in the Concordia alliance with Bolivia and Paraguay, aren't they?"

"No," Roles corrected. "They withdrew last year. They're now part of the New American South with Argentina and Chile."

"What about Brazil? Are they still heading the Formal Union of Latin Central?"

"No, they dissolved the F.U.L.C. before the accords so they could negotiate on their own terms. They're rebuilding under the banner, N.L.C. *New Latin Central.*"

John rubbed his chin. "You know, I was in the Senate Intelligence Committee a short time ago, and I still can't keep track of any of this."

"Your expertise was with the Soviet Union and Europe."

"What's your expertise then?"

"Foreign nations."

"Bit of a large net, isn't it?"

"I don't have any hobbies."

"Well here's the situation," McAndrews interrupted. "The *peace accords* will collapse when Venezuela pulls out. When they do, we can either continue to have Americans there in harm's way, or we can just let the bastards have at it again."

"So what's your advice then?"

"Wasn't that obvious?" McAndrew grunted. "Pull out and let them tear each other apart. We've got our hands full with the European debt negotiations and the collapse of the Soviet Union. We don't stabilize it, then we're going to see a domino effect. Let the South Americans cut each other's throats if they want to."

"You really think that's the best idea when the last conflict killed about five percent of the entire continent?"

"My *best* idea is to not have an alien plague spread into Europe and start killing people. Humans killing each other on the other hand is something I can live with."

"The Chinese are pushing for Venezuela to pull out of the accords," Roles said. "If they do, then the Chinese think it'll be all the easier to get in there and do business with the Venezuelans for those mineral rights. If we leave, the Chinese are going to fill our spot, it's that simple."

"And?" McAndrews frowned. *"Here's a turd in a bag. I wrapped it for you. Don't call us if you get shit on your fingers."* He mocked handing it off. "You don't keep a turd in your pocket just because someone else wants it."

Roles didn't so much as crack a smile. "Despite everything that's going on, I do not believe allowing the Chinese free access to that amount of lithium would be a good idea."

"You know they think the same about us?" McAndrews opened his arms. "All this hard talk about focusing on the real threat, and when it comes down to it, we're still going to be talking about who makes the most money."

"Not money," Roles said. "Lithium is used for smart missiles. Computer chips. CAG. It's for making war. And I'd prefer us to have a ready supply."

"Both of you, take a breath." John made a gesture down with his hands and glanced toward Roles. "It's not our lithium, it's theirs. I'm not about to start taking it from them and provoke a conflict." McAndrews had just begun to smile when John shifted his gaze over to him. "But Roles is right. We can't let China set up shop in there, and regardless of what either of you think, I'm not going to idly stand by as another massive conflict erupts and watch civilians get chewed up if I can stop it."

McAndrews tisked and leaned back in his chair. "What then? We don't have many cards to play here."

"Roles, is the USS Washington still close to the Caribbean?"

"Close enough."

"Order a stealth arrowhead to do a flyover of the president's mansion. See that it's close enough to blow the windows out. We're going to make sure the president understands we intend to stay a little longer and that he reconsider his stance within the peace accords."

"Yes, sir."

"Little harsh." McAndrews widened his eyes. "President Warren made a promise that America wasn't going to be doing anymore big dick diplomacy."

"I'm not President Warren, and like you said, we have bigger problems in hand."

McAndrews shrugged. "Got it."

"Now if that's it from you two, then I've got to give a speech in a few hours."

"One other thing, sir." Roles held up a finger. "I wanted to give you a report on your daughter."

John shifted his weight, and his neck stiffened.

"She's okay, isn't she?"

Roles nodded his head. "Of course sir, she was just in a successful operation to retake Warsaw. I'm told she was instrumental. I'm just making sure to keep you informed."

"All right, then what is it?"

"The reports coming in are that she's turning back much of the enemy advance. And while we still don't seem to understand much about her abilities, we have determined that she seemed to work in an optimal capacity when placed in cryo each night."

"Cryo?" John frowned. "That makes her optimal? Doesn't it have hazy effects and memory loss?"

"The older models did. The newer ones have minimal side effects for most people, and they keep it at short durations. You should be proud of her."

John nodded his head. "I'm. . ."

He was at a loss for words. Proud? Was that how he felt? He'd have her back here and at home in a heartbeat if he thought he could.

"I am."

"I'll leave you to it then, Mr. President." Roles nodded to both John and McAndrews and headed out.

A FEW HOURS slipped by and John rehearsed his speech with Cora while Eli played with his toy cars on the floor. He'd already rehearsed it in front of a few aides, and McAndrews had even given him the thumbs up. But he trusted Cora more than any of them.

John cleared his throat and read from his datapad.

"My fellow Americans."

He went through the entire speech, with the only other sound being Eli's zooming noises with his toys.

Cora was silent as she listened.

John finished and looked at her. She stared back. Finally he shrugged and asked, "What do you think?"

"It's a speech alright." She glanced away.

"What does that mean?"

"It means, it's a speech." She shrugged her shoulders. "I'm sure the writer spent a lot of time on it."

"He told me it took him two days to write."

"Sounds like it."

"Cora, you know more than anyone I'm squeezed for time here. I've eaten dinner with you once in the last two weeks, and haven't slept a full night since assuming office. I'd rather you not speak to me in code."

"What I'm saying is that as a speech, it's nice, but it's not you John. It's not John Winters."

"I don't know what that means."

"John, what's your approval rating?"

"Honestly, I don't even—"

"It's thirty six percent. It was forty one last week. You're looking to be in the twenties if we keep this up much longer."

"What does that have to do with this speech?"

"Your approval rating while a member of the Senate was eighty three percent, John. Everyone liked you. They counted on you to tell the truth and stand up for what was right. To be the moral authority of Congress. To give them the hard medicine no one else would. *Eighty three percent.*"

"I'm not in Congress anymore, Cora. I'm president of the United States, and I've half lost my mind. Not to mention I go live in forty five minutes." He gleaned at his watch.

"Oh, so you just wanted me to tell you I liked it then?" Cora gave a big, plastic smile. "It's wonderful. You'll do great." The smile fell off. "Now that I told you what you wanted to hear, here's what I *actually* think." She pointed at the script. "Throw that in the garbage, and go on there and be John Winters."

"Cora, how in the *hell* do I be John Winters?"

"I don't know, I'm not John Winters. *You're* John Winters."

"For God's sake, you're literally the only person in the world that would talk to me this way."

"You're right, and that's why you want my opinion. I'm the only one that would tell you to throw that in the trash and go out there, because here's the truth, John. The American people are scared. *I'm scared.*" Her voice wavered and she smiled for a second to refocus. "And you're not just my husband, you're my president. And I can tell you, no one wants to hear someone else's words coming out of your mouth. They want you to go up there and give them the hard medicine and then tell them what we're going to do about it."

John laughed under his breath and shook his head. "So you want me to come up with a new speech in—" He looked at his watch. "Forty three minutes?"

"I want you to take a breath, remember who you are, and what you stand for, and I want you to go out there and tell the American people the reality. That way they know who is in charge and that they can believe you."

WHEN JOHN LEFT Cora to go to the East room, he took the speech with him. He read it over a few more times and even took a pen out to make a few notes. Under entirely normal circumstances, he might have requested more edits, but there was a shortage of manpower and time, so he had to take things as they were.

When the hour neared, he walked up to the podium and all the reporters in the room fell silent. A teleprompter was set up just ahead, and the operators had scrambled to incorporate John's latest notes into the speech. The man gave him a thumbs up and John tipped his head to him.

It started to roll and John began, "My fellow Americans." The words scrolled across the screen but John's throat tightened up.

The words continued to go as John stared at it.

The operator spun his finger in a *wind-back* motion and shrugged at John.

John ignored him and shifted his gaze to look out at the reporters. Tomorrow, half of these people would be writing headlines with harsh language about how incompetent he was, and the other half would say the same but with nicer words.

This speech was for them. It was how a president was supposed to talk.

It wasn't John. He might be the president, but in reality, he never would have won it in a fair contest. He never would have bowed to the special interest, or said the right things to rally a coalition into his voter base.

John never should have been president. He'd placated to no one, and owed no favors. He wasn't who the American people would have selected.

But here he was.

John looked away from the reporters and past the teleprompter, he stared directly into the camera.

He wasn't speaking to the reporters anymore. He was speaking to the people.

This shoe fit more comfortably than the other.

"I have some news that will be upsetting."

ROLES WAS in a game of cat and mouse, though he was pretty sure he had the mouse cornered. It was hard to be certain when playing the shadow game, but he'd been playing it for years.

He was an expert.

At the moment, he was lounging in his seat. Of course, there was always work to be done, but Roles was getting up there in years, and who knew? He could die from a heart attack tomorrow. Then who would drink all of his booze?

The little moments in life were the ones you needed to cherish.

He filled his glass and turned on the TV. This could be work after all. Call it research.

He waited to see what the Venezuelan president was going to say on TV.

But the time came and passed.

There was no such appearance.

Guess he's busy buying new windows.

Roles checked the time and sipped from his glass as he pulled up Moller's latest report.

Interesting details.

But the time came that John Winters' speech was coming on, and Roles decided it was time for another drink.

He filled his glass as John Winters' voice played from the TV.

"My fellow Americans."

John trailed off.

Roles brought the glass to his lips and froze in place as the silence extended for a few uncomfortable seconds.

Well, this is awkward.

Something shifted in John's stance and posture. Among other things, Roles was an expert on body language, and he could always notice the subtle changes.

Hmm. I didn't think he had the spine for it.

Roles wasn't wrong often. He smiled as he listened.

It was nice to be surprised every now and then.

His phone buzzed on his desk and he picked it up.

An encrypted message came through.

BREAKOUTS IN EUROPEAN FEDERATION, AFRICA, AND SOUTH ASIAN ALLIANCE.

Roles put his phone down and exhaled loudly through his nose.

He supposed some surprises were better than others.

THE CRONUX LIVED A HARSH EXISTENCE. Born from the Mother's eggs, as they hatched, each brood would feed upon one another until the strongest survived. Those strong enough to break the eggs first typically savaged their brothers.

First born.

They were chosen by the Mother, made whole in her desires, and sent upon other worlds in the name of her hunger.

The brood died so that the strongest would live.

This was not the way of the Archon.

Three kings.

Three crowns.

Three to rule the world.

It was this way on many worlds, in many realities, for this was the will of the Mother.

But not here.

The Arab Archon had come through the gate last.

The youngest of his brothers.

But with an innate understanding of war, he broke the men there and pushed them back. Though he was an Archon, and strength beyond comparison to others of his race, he was weak by the standards of his brothers.

The last of his brood to break the egg.

He was not strong, but he was wise.

When enough blood had spilled, and the men pushed beyond reach of the gate, the Arab Archon had knelt down and reached for his brothers.

Three kings. Three crowns. Three to rule the world.

But there was sickness within the hive mind. It made the hive mind *thick* and threatened to corrupt the Arab Archon.

The Archon were supposed to connect, to build a will and coalition amongst themselves in the Mother's name.

Instead, only one brother was there, the Jade Archon, and though the hive mind was not a physical place, his brother whispered as if in fear that another was listening.

Our brother has changed. He said this without words but feeling and understanding, for the Archon did not speak in words.

He is scarred. He is insane.

Fear him.

The Arab Archon felt the sickness within the hive mind now. It crawled as if it had legs.

The scarred Archon.

What was there to do when a mad god came for the weakest among his brothers? Such was the way of the Archon, that he did not consider going through the gate.

He simply waited.

There, near the pulsing glow of the gate, with the love of the Mother flowing upon him, the Arab Archon knelt, and focused on his children and his loyal servants.

Strong, no, but he was wise.

And he refused to die easily.

THE SCARRED ARCHON bounded onto the streets of Tehran. A vicious excitement flowed through his veins.

He leapt into the air and his wings extended out with a single powerful thrust. It hurled him far and wide across the battlefield and into the lines of the enemy.

He collided onto the ground in the center of his brother's horde. The force of his impact knocked his enemies back, but they came at him immediately.

A hundred mouths widened, their fangs glistening, and they came for his flesh.

The horde had not expected him, but they reacted quickly.

They came for his body.

The Archon fought without form or tactics, but a beast enraged. He threw his body about and slashed his claws in all directions. One blow crushed the head of an enemy, knocking its body down to be trampled by its brothers. He swung his tail out and cleaved through a weak framed cronux. A banshee screamer leapt at him and he cleaved it in two with a strike from his open hand.

One large, four legged beast barreled into him and took the Archon off his feet as the beast's mouth snapped on him. One of its large, crooked teeth skewered the Archon, and its back molars ground his foot.

The Archon felt the bones in his foot crush as the sharp tooth dug into his waist, making dark blood pool in the wound.

The Archon snarled and dragged his claw down across the creature's face, opening lines of wounds that exposed pink muscle.

The creature, unabated, chewed and ran. They smashed into a wall and the Archon was pinned to the stone. The creature's jaw ground back and forth trying to chew the Archon's leg off.

But the Archon got a hand into its mouth and dug his claws into the roof of the beast's mouth. With sharp fingers, he cut the tender flesh.

The beast backpedaled and swung its head back and forth, somehow trying to shake the pain away, but it was too late. The Archon cut through the beast's mouth and into its brain. He grabbed onto the nerve stems fitted into its skull and yanked hard enough that they ripped free.

The beast stumbled and fell and the Archon shoved its jaws open wide enough that the bone snapped, and came out of its mouth with a large fist full of brains.

He threw the slop at one rushing cronux and hit it in the face. The moment of confusion stopped it mid run and the Archon darted forward, and cleaved its head off with one blow.

More came and he whipped his tail into them, the sharp point cutting and piercing with ease.

A circle of flesh closed in on the Archon, dozens bit at him, and as he killed wave after wave, they continued to flow over the dead.

Standing on top of their broken bodies, the Archon crouched and leapt. He went into the air even as hands on the ground grasped at him.

The Archon landed on a building and a squad of human soldiers were there, firing down at the cronux.

A nearby soldier was caught by surprise and hesitated. The Archon snatched him and tossed him aside to the horde beneath.

Another soldier turned a power mounted placement gun onto the Archon and fired.

Thick, heavy shells smashed into the Archon, making pain rattle through his body as he fell back. Chunks of his flesh and body blew off while the gun pounded loudly and shook the entire roof. After three heavy shots, the Archon darted to the side as the gun twisted to follow him. He leapt into the air, and the gun arched high, but it wasn't fast enough. He came down on top of it, and the impact made the operator stumble and fall off the roof into the open hands of the enemy horde beneath.

One soldier turned his back to the city and aimed his rifle. He fired at the Archon to little consequence, the bullets little more than pecks against the Archon's flesh.

A large cronux from the Archon's brother's horde walked by on stalk legs. A multi-faced creature with stalk arms, with no care for the Archon, it grabbed the soldier from behind and shoved the man into its mouth. It chewed as the soldier screamed, and his armor crunched in its jaws.

It twisted its body and exposed an unfed face. Its slender arm snapped out toward the Archon.

He leapt into the air and came down on the top of its head.

The Archon's feet dug its claws in, as the creature's head was greasy and slick, and filled with bristly hair that made it hard to hold.

Its slender arms came up and reached for the Archon but he moved quickly. He dug his hand down into its scalp to get a grip and twisted his back to let his tail snake up.

It slammed down into the creature's head. All of the creature's many faces groaned and it spit up the half chewed soldier, sending him down into the horde.

The Archon roared and smashed his tail down twice more until it cut deep into the creature.

The monster stumbled around while frantically reaching for the Archon, but he dug his tail in and extended his wings.

Two powerful thrusts from his wings and the creature went uneven and collapsed across the battle line and into the scarred Archon's horde.

The Archon's children flowed over it, biting pieces off its oily flesh.

The Archon pulled his bloody tail out and threw himself into the air again, intent for more blood.

THERE WAS SOME POINT, around midday, when the Arab Archon opened his eyes and stepped away from his connection with the battle.

He was not strong, but he was wise, and he knew that he was losing.

And his brother, insane and malignant, would kill him.

It did not pain him to die, it only pained him to know that he had failed the Mother. That she had given him purpose, and he had but taken a small step in that direction.

And now he waited.

Hours might have passed, he didn't know. The station he was in rattled from some mighty explosion above and the electricity went out.

But the gate continued. When they gave their instructions across the void to the humans, they determined backup powers that would keep it from failing.

Now the vibrant green glow of the gate cast a light upon him as it bubbled and popped with energy.

His brother came alone.

The Arab Archon felt that within the hive mind.

He took a seat and waited. There would be no final struggle. His brother, though savage, had proven himself superior in war.

The scarred Archon entered into the room, and the green glow of the gate shined on him.

The scarred Archon looked first to the gate, and then to him. The scarred Archon had changed. His body was rippled with muscle, and tips of wings protruded over his shoulders.

The Arab Archon would soon die, but he was curious and he wanted to know

Why?

He asked in their language through the hive mind.

His brother answered, but he did so with human words.

"Because I can."

KEVIN WAS the first to suggest it, then everything snapped together for Miles

This woman was a clone, just like the ones he'd seen in Moscow, but she was damaged.

If there were healthy ones, then they had departed.

They left her behind.

"Fucking hell." Miles put his hands behind his head and stood up. The woman leaned her head back and the eye on her neck rolled around to look up at Miles. *"Why does it keep staring at me?"*

"How will we even know which ones are people and which ones aren't?" Kevin asked.

"Mate, that's what we're here to figure out." He gestured down to the woman. *"Where the shadows are deepest, the secrets are darkest,* and all that right?"

Endo leaned up. "You stay here and see what you can find out. I'll go back to the truck and make sure things are secured."

"Wait, why the hell do you get to be the one that leaves?" Miles said.

Endo said nothing, he only grabbed the handle of his sword and pulled it from his forearm guard.

"Shit, he does have a sword," Kevin said, his eyes going wide.

"Give me the walkie." Endo put his hand out and Miles gave it to him. Endo made a few adjustments on it and handed it back. He tapped his helmet. "Report to me if you hear anything."

Miles tucked the walkie talkie's clip onto his belt. "All right, all right."

"I'll be fast," Endo said and then took off in the direction of the trucks. His CAG helped him move faster than any man possibly could.

"Nuts to all this," Miles said looking back down at the woman. "What the hell am I supposed to do with this thing?"

"We're supposed to figure out how to determine if they're alien or not."

Miles closed his eyes and took a deep breath. "I know *that*. What I mean is where the hell do we begin?"

"You're the expert, not me."

"I'm an expert at bullshitting, Kevin. It helps me get morons like yourself to give me their money and to occasionally find a woman who will sleep with me. I don't know anything about real alien autopsies. We've been over this, keep up."

"It wouldn't be an autopsy because it's not dead. You think we should kill it first or something?"

"Honest to God, I wouldn't even know where to begin." Miles dared a look down at the woman.

She stared up at him and widened her mouth like a fish, the eye stared at Miles before trying to blink.

Miles winced. "*Dammit*, it gets me each time. You'd think I'd be over it by now."

Kevin shook his head and put his hands on his hips. "When you saw them before, what did you see?"

Miles nodded his head. "Some ugly woman crawling out of an egg. Real mean bitch. Wanted to shred my face and all that."

"How's that help? You're not saying anything useful."

"I was just telling you what happened! She slithered out of an egg and—" Miles looked up for a moment. A sudden realization waving over him. He rubbed his chin and looked at the woman.

"What is it, did you think of something?"

"Ehh, I suppose. You're not going to like it though."

Kevin fanned his arms out. "Let's hear it."

"Saw two of them mate." He held up fingers. "Both naked as a young babe. Man and a woman. But here's the gist." He made a wave across his crotch. "Not a cock or cunt among them. Flat as a barbie doll. Pubeless bastards, too."

Kevin made a face then. "Are you saying what I think you're saying then?"

Miles gave him a sympathetic look and nodded, then together they looked down at the woman who was staring at them with all four eyes.

"I think we need to take a peek at her naughty bits."

ENDO RAN EVEN though doing so made his intestinal pain all the worse. He felt like he could throw up.

Instead he choked it down and went faster.

All the years Endo had spent training to ignore pain, to go without sleep, to suffer in silence. . . It was all flushed away.

The snake writhing inside him had distracted him. It made him dumb and dull.

He should have seen something like this coming.

How could he have been so foolish?

He came over the crest of a hill and saw the trucks still there and people milling about. Some were making trades and others cooking on small fires.

He wasn't too late.

Endo slowed and sheathed his sword. There was no need to make a panic or to set anyone off.

One of the leaders of the group looked up at Endo and spoke in Russian.

"Where are the others? Did you find anything?"

"They're still there," Endo said, his voice coming through the external speakers on the CAG helmet. Endo looked amongst the group.

The town was empty. One woman was there.

There should have been more.

Some of these people were not who they seemed.

"But did you find anything?" the man repeated.

Endo closed the gap to him and pushed the clasp on his helmet. It puffed out air and then rose up, he pulled it off.

"Where are the new arrivals?" Endo asked.

"They're mixing about and trading goods. A few more travelers have arrived since you've returned. We hoped you could find food to accommodate all of them."

Endo gave the man a sharp look. "Separate the new people from the old."

"Why? What are you looking for?" the man asked.

Endo shook his head. "I don't know yet."

"FLIP YOU FOR IT?"

Miles had made the offer, and Kevin provided the coin.

"My lucky coin," he said as he pulled it out of his pocket. Miles took a look at it, as no one carried hard money these days.

It was an antique.

"You call?" Kevin asked.

"Heads."

Kevin flipped it into the air and smacked one hand down on the coin, catching it on his palm.

He lifted his hand just half an inch and peeked.

"Now don't be a peckerhead, let me see it," Miles groaned.

Kevin lifted his hand.

Tails.

"Shit on that. Your *lucky* coin and all. Cheating bastard."

Kevin shrugged.

"If she has an eye up her arse, then I'm *fucking* done for, mate."

Miles leaned up and patted his pockets. "You got a pen or something? I don't want to go digging around there with my fingers."

Kevin pulled a pen out of his pocket and handed it over.

Miles took the pen and looked it over. He pressed the button on the back of it twice making the tip pop in and out of its sleeve. He turned it over in his hand and read the brand, then clicked it two more times.

"What? Does it need to be a certain kind of pen?"

"Just working the nerve up." Miles sighed. "All the others I saw were naked. Why do you suppose this one is dressed?"

Kevin shrugged. "Why does she have multiple eyes? Who knows."

"Right." Miles nodded and clicked the pen twice more. He looked down at the woman and she had her mouth opened in a wide—oh!—face with the eyeball staring at him.

"Say one thing about her, she's docile. Suppose that's in my favor when checking if she has a minge."

"You're making too big of a deal about it. How's it any worse than all the nasty stuff you've done on your TV show? I saw you eat a cow testicle before."

"I was lit, and the testicle was boiled, mate. Oh, and I was getting paid. Money has always been an inspiring thing for me

"I've got a dollar?"

"Shut up. And while I've certainly talked my way into more than a few pairs of panties in my life, it was always with permission. Just seems wrong to go digging around where I wasn't invited."

"Oh, right. You're upset that she didn't give you permission, and it's not that she might have an eyeball up her arse. Think of it this way. I used to work in a veterinarian office. Sometimes we had to look to see if the animal was male or female, no one asked, and the animal didn't care." Kevin pointed down at the woman. "*She won't care.*"

Miles nodded his head. Dammit to hell, he felt lame. Kevin was right. He'd done *far* more disgusting things than this. Far more. Maybe.

"Just getting in the right headspace." He took a deep breath. "All right, let's do it before I change my mind." Miles walked around to her back and used the pen to hook her dress and lift it.

No underwear.

No vagina.

"Slick as a bowling ball." He let it drop and stepped back. "That's how you can tell what's what. Need a look at their bits."

"So what? We tell Kota to tell everyone to pull their pants down?"

"I've pulled my cock out for worse." Miles lifted his eyebrows. "Little frontal nudity never hurt no one. Specially if it saves you from getting your face eaten." He fished the walkie talkie out. "Here, mate, you make the call. I don't want to tell Kota that he start looking at everyone's bits over there." He tossed it.

Kevin caught it and frowned. He pressed the button.

"Kota, you there?"

A few seconds later a voice came on.

"I'm here."

"We found a way to tell the aliens. You see, they uhh. They don't have penises. Peni?" He let go of the button and looked at Miles. "What's the plural word for penis?"

"Fucking, uhh." Miles frowned but nodded. "Believe it's penises."

"That sounds weird, though, right?"

Miles nodded in agreement.

Kevin pushed the button again. "Yeah, no penises, or like, a vagina. I mean." Kevin raised his shoulders and made a face at Miles. "No pubic hair either. Hey, maybe they don't have armpit hair, right? That might be better than looking at their junk."

A few seconds ticked by. *"Affirmative."*

"I guess, we'll, uhh." Kevin shrugged again and puckered his lips. "We'll keep looking around?"

"I'll call if I see anything. Endo out."

"Hell, way to cut to the chase there." Miles shook his head. "Real sprint to the finish."

"Listen." Kevin made a slash with his finger across the air. "I'm a computer guy, I'm not an *aliens with no dicks* guy."

"You still got that bottle?" Miles pointed at Kevin's bag. "I need a swig for sure to take the—"

Something snapped loudly next to Miles' feet. He shifted to look.

The woman's arms had cracked backward at the elbow.

"The hell did she do that for?" Miles gaffed and took a step back.

One foot twisted like the hand of a clock. The skin tore on her foot and her leg cracked. Then her foot fell off, far easier than it should have been.

She slid the stump from the restraint.

"Shit!" Miles grabbed Kevin's sleeve and pulled him back along with him.

The woman slithered beneath her bounds, working her way in them. Her stump leg slammed down into the ground.

She'd gone from being docile to active like someone flipped a switch.

Her shoulders cracked and her bound hands came together like a tree trunk. Her head crunched and rolled back to act like some kind of leg. Blood pooled beneath her dress near her stomach and then tentacles pierced through it.

"Go, go!" Miles yelled and ran away.

The woman dragged with a startling speed across the dirt. She moved like a living table, her back aimed down and using her head and arms as another set of legs. It was awkward and unnerving, but she was fast. The tentacles flailed out around her stomach threatening to snatch Miles and Kevin.

"The car!" Miles pointed and he and Kevin jumped up on the hood of the car and then onto the roof. Miles jumped for the ledge of a building and grabbed onto it. He lifted himself up and turned over.

Kevin bent down to leap when the woman hit the car. She bucked up onto the car with her legs and the flailing tentacles swung around. Kevin jumped and grabbed the ledge and Miles grabbed him, trying to help him up.

One of the woman's tentacles wrapped around Kevin's ankle and pulled.

"Oh shit!" Kevin screamed and stared at Miles with panicked eyes.

"Hold on, mate, just hold on!" Miles ground his teeth and pulled.

The woman came up farther on the car and another tentacle wrapped around Kevin's leg.

That was too much.

Kevin was ripped from Miles' hands and slammed into the roof of the car. The bloody gash in the woman's stomach where the tentacles came from widened like a mouth to pull Kevin in.

Miles stood up, on the roof, frozen in horror as there was nothing he could do but watch his friend be dragged in.

Kevin screamed and lost his grip as he slid down the car.

But there was nothing to do.

Kevin was as good as dead.

But then Miles had one of those moments, where the weight of the world lightened and time slowed. Flashes of Kevin's face came into his mind. The look of the man when they first met. When they went into the Soviet Union. When he told Miles he just wanted to help people.

And when Miles told him he was here for the money.

"You're just an asshole," Miles's ex-wife's voice rang in his ears.

It was true. He was. But Kevin wasn't.

And only one of them deserved what Kevin was about to get.

"You fucking cunt!" Miles bellowed as he went into the air before his mind had worked the plan out. He came down feet first on her, and the sudden weight knocked her back. Her tentacles pulled Kevin fully off the car, but released him.

Miles tumbled down onto the dirt and smacked his face on the ground.

He only had enough time to look back and see the woman's tentacles slither up his leg.

———

ENDO HEARD Kevin's call come in and placed his helmet back on as he watched from a short distance. He talked with Kevin as the new people were cordoned off. He tried to see each carefully. Which were acting strange, which were acting normal. . .

It was hard to tell what *strange* and *normal* were for a human being in the middle of a collapsing nation and alien presence.

One man sat quietly by himself with a distant dull look on his face. Perhaps his family had all died? A woman rocked back and forth on her feet near another, as they whispered words to each other. There were more still, each peculiar in their own way, each strange. What was there to tell the difference in any of them, what could Endo possibly. . .

He stopped.

There was a young, clean shaven man. He was chatting with another man. They both wore heavy clothes.

Endo walked over to them and spoke in Russian. "You." He pointed at the young man.

"*Why?*" the man said, his voice a scratch.

"I won't hurt you, but you have to come with me," Endo insisted.

"*No.*" The man stood his ground.

Endo reached up and grabbed his arm. "You have to—"

His fingers sunk into the muscle. Nothing to grip. Like squeezing a wet balloon.

The man's arm flexed in places where it shouldn't be able to and wrapped down Endo's arm.

"Everyone move!" Endo screamed.

The man shook and his ears fell off and his hair shed in clumps. He moaned and his mouth widened like a snake to swallow prey.

Endo pulled his sword out in a flash and cut through the man's arm, and a second strike through the midsection.

The man's top half collapsed like putty, and his dismembered arm swung back and slapped the ground with a wet slap as it stretched into strands.

The man who had been talking to him was standing too close and those strands snaked onto him. They grabbed the man and the monster gulped onto his leg.

Endo hacked down and took the top of the monster's head off, but it seemed only a mild irritation as he continued to chew on his victim's leg.

Endo slashed again and the creature's arm fell off and quivered on the ground.

The victim screamed as the creature squirmed up his leg. The creature's entire body changed shape and formed tiny, biting mouths.

"Everyone back!" Endo screamed again, but then the nerves on his back tightened.

He looked behind just fast enough to see a man with a mouth three times as large as it should be barrel toward him.

Endo moved with a quickness and the monster went past him and tripped into a cooking pot, spilling its contents and landing in the fire.

The monster shrieked as small fire reached up like gas had been poured on it. Endo moved in quickly and jammed his sword down into the middle of its body, pinning it down.

The monster stretched about like putty, but the sword kept it in place as it flailed and burned.

Endo turned back to the first, and the man it was eating had only a muffled scream now as it went over his face.

Endo dug his fingers into the soft flesh, and the creature's eyes rolled back to stare at him. With startling speed, it moved up his arms and across his body, leaving the half chewed victim to fall on his knees and collapse to the ground.

Lights flashed in Endo's helmet warning of danger and a breach as the creature started to tighten. His CAG would break.

Blinded with the creature rolling over his helmet, Endo took a few steps to where he knew another fire was and jumped inside.

The creature writhed and squirmed on him, but Endo's fingers tightened and held it in place.

His radio came alive again with Kevin's voice.

"Help, we need help!"

Endo ground his teeth and held the squirming monster as he spoke.

"Kill it with fire."

THE CREATURE'S tentacles snaked up Miles's leg as he tried to crawl away. He felt it ooze up his ankle and start to tighten.

"Shit!"

Miles worked at his belt buckle and unzipped his pants. As the tentacle slithered up his leg, Miles kicked the pants loose, and his shoe sucked off. He bounced onto his feet in his underwear.

With one shoe on, he went on a dead run as the creature gobbled his pants. A moment later it realized there was no meat and started chasing Miles.

"Shit—shit—shit!"

"Back here!" Kevin yelled.

Miles shot a look back and saw Kevin on the ground near the car.

"Get to the roof again!" Kevin pointed but ran behind the building.

Miles looped and sprinted while the half formed woman galloped behind him, like some horrible cartoon demon.

Miles groaned as his bare foot stepped on a rock, but he ground his teeth and jumped on the hood once more and hopped to the roof of the car. His shoeless foot slid on the metal and he smacked the roof.

"Fuck," he huffed and looked back to see the creature closing in.

He got up to his feet again as the creature thumped into the car and hissed. Miles stepped onto the roof and jumped up to the ledge. He pulled himself over again.

"Kevin?" Miles looked around and didn't see him, but heard the monster hiss below.

Miles peeked over the edge and saw a burning rag stuffed into the car's gas pump. The creature was just below him, and its tentacles reached up for his face. Its mouth widened and screamed.

Miles rolled back over and put his hands on his ears.

There was a loud explosion and fire puffed up near the edge. The creature beneath them shrieked and moaned.

Miles opened his eyes and took his hands off his ears. He sat for a moment and listened to the crackle of the flame.

After a few seconds' pause, Miles rolled over the edge and looked down again. A fire was coming out of the car and the alien was cooking on top of it.

"Hey!" Kevin waved from some distance away. He gave Miles a thumbs up. "We got it."

Miles nodded with a pained smile and laid his head back down.

"You need some new pants?" Kevin yelled.

"Yeah," Miles said weakly. "And a new pair of underwear."

ERKIN KAHN WOKE UP CONFUSED. His whole body was chilled and he was in a bed of foggy pink liquid. He struggled to find a way out, but as he pressed his hands up he touched glass.

Blurred images of people moved around on the other side of the glass.

He panicked and shook in desperation. A moment later there was a loud beep and the hatch to the bed rose.

Erkin sat up from the bed with a jolt and puked a mouthful of the liquid.

Doctors in full gowns and masks stood over the hatch of the cryo bed and placed an oxygen mask onto his face. He puked again inside the mask, and the furious, confused team shouted back and forth as they pulled the mask back off.

Erkin's eyes were blurred and he wiped them away, but no sooner had he started to take a breath, they put the mask back on him.

His eyes widened as he took a breath of purified air and the people grabbed onto him and lifted him out of the bed, careless as they soaked their gowns in the process.

Thick gel leaked off his cold, naked body, and the doctors

inspected him immediately. Speaking to each other in Mandarin too fast for Erkin to follow.

He had terrible bruises over his body from the beatings he had endured at the camp, and a heal-fast cast had been placed over his arm where it had apparently been broken. Strong, nutrient-rich synthetic skin weave bandages were placed around his ribs where several were damaged from clubs.

Erkin got a look at himself in the mirror and saw that one eye was completely blood red and likely dead.

It was hard to remember precisely why that was, or what he was doing here. There were vague impressions, like the beatings, but all other memories seemed to pull away when he reached for them.

The doctors moved him toward a gurney, and he sat down as they poured over him, checking his health readings.

The memories started to trickle back.

A cold dark room.

A lit cigarette.

A man in gold framed glasses with a wide, knowing grin.

Wu.

"You can help us, Erkin," Wu had said, seated at his desk. *"You can kill the enemies of China."*

What had Erkin said? What had been his response? He didn't remember.

"Your family, Erkin?" Wu's words still echoed. *"We will bring your family. And we will build you a house within the center of Beijing, rivaled only by Chairman Zhao's. Kill our enemies and become a hero of the People's Republic. You will be greatly rewarded."*

For some reason Erkin remembered Wu taking the cigarette out of his mouth and stabbing it into a gray, glass ashtray. The cigarette smoldered there in the dark office, and Wu leaned close.

"Do we have a deal?" Wu's gold framed glasses gleamed from the soft light in the room.

Erkin didn't remember what he said, or what he agreed to. He only knew that he was here.

"Suit him for CAG," a man overlooking the doctors said.

Erkin was guided into a wheelchair and sat down. They pushed him along the way and he looked at the walls.

"Where's my wife?" Erkin asked without even meaning to.

Everyone ignored him as they talked amongst themselves, and though Erkin knew the language, his brain was still fogged from the cryo to understand.

He knew this and closed his eyes, and tried to focus.

Within his mind he stepped to the house he was building, but it now lay in rubble.

And there, at the base of the house, he turned and looked across the horizon.

Was he alone? Where was his wife?

He knew this place wasn't real, but it was real enough, and he needed it. He needed his family.

He only had to conjure them.

But at that moment, as he decided to call for his wife, he realized something odd.

He couldn't remember her name.

And though there were flashes of her long black hair and beautiful eyes. . .

He couldn't remember her face.

"No!" Erkin burst up out of the wheelchair and collapsed onto the floor, making the whole entourage panic.

"What's her name?" Erkin screamed as loud as he could. He grabbed an orderly by the collar and pulled the woman close, her face red and panicked. *"I can't remember her name!"*

Erkin bellowed as someone grabbed him by the neck and pulled him back. Another person wrenched onto his arm and held it still while a woman ran quickly to him with a needle in hand. Erkin kicked her in the leg hard enough that it broke her knee and she fell back with a tortured scream.

Another man snatched her needle from the floor and jammed it into Erkin's arm as he wrestled.

The world darkened.

"Erkin?" a voice said, pulling him from the darkness. *"Erkin, I thought we had a deal?"*

Erkin opened his eyes. He was in the same dark room.

Another cigarette, stabbed and smoldering in the ashtray.

Golden frames rested on Wu's face.

"Where?" Erkin asked.

"We trust that we still have a deal, yes? Perhaps it was the cryo sleep that fogged your mind. Everyone reacts differently, and it was your first time. We believed it was supposed to focus you, but it appears it did not. We will not try it again."

Erkin rubbed his face and focused his eyes.

Wu sat across from him again.

"I can't think," Erkin said.

Wu grinned, his gold-rimmed glasses shining from the light once more. "You don't need to think. We think for you. You only need to do what we tell you. That is best."

"What do you need me to do?" Erkin's voice cracked. He tightened his eyes closed and fought to clear his mind.

Wu frowned. "We've gone over this. You will kill the enemies of China, and you will be rewarded. But first, you must go and be suited for CAG. Then we will deploy you in some small combat zones before we—"

"Where is my wife?" His mind started to clear.

"In good hands," Wu said. "She will be safer when you have completed your work and she's joined you in Beijing." Wu continued. "You will be deployed in contained zones so that we can analyze your abilities, and then you will be targeted toward the hive's nest in Beijing."

"I don't know what's happening. I don't know what you want me to do."

Wu's smile slipped off. "As I said, you don't *need* to know. We will think for you. Your life now has but one purpose. Kill those I tell you to kill."

"My wife, what is her name?"

Wu's lips tightened. "As we sit here and speak, an alien presence spreads within China. It has nearly consumed Beijing, and will soon spread throughout the country. If Beijing falls, your wife too will fall as with all of China. Do you love your wife, Erkin?"

"Yes," he nodded.

Wu set a picture down and slid it over the desk.

The picture was of a horned beast with the same frame and design of a man, though it was naked and had no sex.

"Then do what is right." Wu's grin returned. "Help us kill the devil."

"BECAUSE I CAN."

Those were the final words the Archon offered his brother before he snatched him by the throat and pulled him to the ground.

His nails dug into his brother's tender throat as he struggled. But his brother was weak.

The scarred Archon was not.

Amongst screams and thrashing, the scarred Archon pressed his nails into brother's scalp and peeled the top layer off. The bone cracked loudly and snapped.

The exposed, white brain pulsed with blood and energy, doubling as a third heart.

With his brother's scream trickling off into an agonized moan, the Archon clawed out chunks of the brain and stuffed it into his mouth.

As he chewed the white chunks, pink juice leaked between his teeth and ran down his fingers. Each bite sent electricity through his veins, and new worlds and ideas opened into him.

And he became more than he was.

He hissed as the energy sizzled through him and let his brother's body sag on his grip. The brains dribbled out onto the floor like wet slop.

He approached the gate, dragging his brother who left a wet smear, and stood before the green glow.

Vague impressions of the Fathers moved there, ever careful of their delicate work in service to the Mother.

The Archon took one step to the gate and felt a chill.

A darkness passed over him, a thought from somewhere within the gate.

Was it his Mother's whispers?

You have sinned.

Or were they only imagined?

Heretic.

He wasn't sure, but how could she not love him if he'd proven his strength?

There was much he didn't know, and much he didn't understand.

But if there was one truth, it was that his mother's call for kingdom was religion, and her hunger was faith.

"I will take this world," he said with human words to the glowing gate, the shadows of the Fathers still moving beyond it. "And I will give it to you."

He waited for an answer.

None came.

This gate had been his brother's; it was attuned to him. His brother, now dead, had used it to speak to the other world and to bring more from it.

Would the Mother allow him to take it, even with her son's corpse in his hand? Even if he would only use it to kill his other brother?

"Come."

He spoke the word, a command for control.

He waited.

A new shadow formed at the gate. It lumbered forward.

Its foot cut through the green fire of the gate as it stepped inside.

The creature was neither powerful or wise—it was simply *more*.

The Archon had received his answer.

Her hunger was eternal.

And he was her son.

WHEN THE ARCHON came up to the surface, he dragged his brother's body in hand.

The fighting had ended, and the defeated enemy horde now bowed in surrender and shame.

The scarred Archon threw his brother's body forward, and small cronux rushed in a frenzy to feast upon it.

The scarred Archon fanned his wings out and walked. His horde howled in praise; the other cowered in fear.

His brother's Janissary was shuffled to the front and dumped at the Archon's feet.

The Janissary was wounded, and a stump was all that remained of one of his arms. Blood p\

]-9876t5REDESXZSUMPED OUT OF IT, and he held his hand up in submission and bowed his head.

The Archon reached down and grabbed him by the chin, and lifted the Janissary's face up. He had grown eyes, but one was plucked out. Now all that remained was a wet hole in his face, while the other eye stared in fear.

He was submissive, and fearful.

He would be obedient.

But he was also weak.

The Archon placed his open hand across the Janissary's face, and all the horde quieted.

He squeezed his fingers as the Janissary squirmed and batted at the Archon's hand with his wounded limbs. With ease, the Archon lifted him into the air and off his feet, then hurled the Janissary into a crowd. He landed in an open patch on the ground, but the frenzied horde fell upon him and ravaged his body as the Archon strained his back and spoke in human words.

"Eat the dead," he told the defeated horde. "Follow me."

His mind stretched over theirs, and they too buzzed with fear and confusion.

But he wouldn't kill them.

No, not when there was still so much work to do.

He settled his reins upon them and they joined him within the hive mind.

With full control, the Archon turned his eyes back north.

The gate and the horde were not all he desired.

He could feel the woman once more.

Alice Winters.

Her presence sent quakes through the hive mind, and with the Archon gone, she had destroyed many.

The Archon knelt low and then burst into the air. His wings unfolded and he surged through the air in flight.

Below him, the horde flowed from the city, with scant few breaking away to hunt survivors, as was their way.

The Archon would have *Alice Winters* soon, and he was not willing to wait.

———————————

WORM HAD FLOWED into the water, and as an engine of evolution, his body changed and ripened to the conditions.

No longer able to burrow through the ground, he grew small flaps and swam.

He encountered a large animal in the sea, and it tried to evade him.

His tentacles sucked it in, and he chewed off parts of it while the water turned red with blood and white, shredded flesh floated near him.

The blood only attracted others, vicious things with teeth and large mouths, but Worm devoured them too.

But one creature, he only grabbed and plunged his teeth inside its flesh, and injected it with parasites.

He released it and the infected creature went on its way with a new mission and purpose.

This war would not be fought only on land.

It would now be fought in the seas.

He pulled back and swam again, and he had to travel a great distance, so he moved quickly and did not stop for long.

The seas seemed endless though, and though Worm was a thing of dull wits, he did grow bored.

A fat edge was above him in the water. Was it a ship? He'd seen such things before from the beaches. With a touch of curiosity, he popped up alongside it.

"Oh fuck, what is that?"

Someone in a yellow coat atop of the ship screamed.

Worm bellowed and opened his mouth. Tentacles reached out and snatched the man off the deck and pulled him in. Worm swallowed him whole.

Not content with the simple meal, Worm sank into the water and then surged to the top to hurl his wet bulk onto the deck of the ship. People shouted and screamed as Worm crushed the deck. He held his head up high and looked about. Spying people clustered in a cabin, he moaned his mouth open once more and the tentacles swam out, shattering glass and reaching for the people.

A few screamers were snagged and pulled into Worm's awaiting jaws, but others retreated and ran farther in where Worm couldn't get them.

He supposed it was hard to get them in the ship, and he couldn't move well with his fins and nothing to kick off of, so Worm squirmed on the deck for a moment before he slid back into the water.

Frustrated, he smashed his face into the bottom of the boat until it turned over. One man fell into the water, and Worm gulped him whole.

He could have stayed and eaten the entire ship, but he had important work ahead of him.

JENNY CASEY HAD SPENT the morning yawning. She worked in an office, and all day everyone talked about how the world was going to hell.

Hell or not, she still wanted her vacation.

She was supposed to go on vacation yesterday, but they called her in today.

"Please? It'll just be a half day. You'll be out by noon!"

Half day or not, that meant this day was shot. She'd been planning every moment of every day when she was supposed to be working. This threw a wrench in things. She was going to see a movie with her boyfriend and have a nice dinner out in uptown Manhattan, but no, Wendy's son was sick so she needed the day off.

"Jenny, can you send me the details for the Hensler account?"

"Sure, sure, just give me fifteen minutes."

She could have done it in five, but she spent the other ten browsing the web deciding what she was going to do with the rest of her spoiled day.

The weather was still nasty, but she decided as soon as she got off, she'd go for a stroll along the beach. New York had beautiful beaches, and it had been a long time since she'd taken a stroll on one.

But it was just her today. When she called things off with her boyfriend, she told him just to go meet one of his friends and have the day to himself. No need for both of them to waste the day, right?

So when she got off, she put her breather in. It wasn't recommended to walk through town without a breather anymore since they correlated the poor air quality with lung cancer.

Day or night, the glowing pink neon lights of the city flashed, and Jenny walked under them on her ninety minute walk to the beach.

She didn't mind the exercise, but it was a pain in the ass with the breather over her face.

It was nice when she got to the open skies of the beach and she could take it off.

Of course, doctors recommended keeping it on even here, as the air pollution stretched some ways out of the city, but she supposed a few hours of exposure would be fine.

She pulled it off her face and stretched her arms out to feel the sun as she looked over the sea.

It was a tinge different color than she remembered it as a child—a bit orange—but the mayor promised that was because of the cleanup efforts, and that they would have it back to where people could swim again in the next coming years.

The city was making an effort to clean things up. It brought some small hope to her, that with everything going wrong, things might still end up better.

In the distance, she saw something rise up from the water.

A horrifying, dark-skinned creature with a fleshy pink mouth. Its large eyelids snapped open, and glossy grey eyes looked about.

Jenny's heart nearly froze in her chest.

It dove back into the water and sent a wave that careened into nearby ships making them bob up and down.

She should have run.

Instead she watched.

It came up again next to a large worker boat.

The people there, small to Jenny's eye, screamed and ran.

The creature gave a deep guttural roar that echoed through the air. Tentacles shot from its mouth and snatched the people off the boat and pulled them into its mouth.

The creature went up and swung back and forth before diving into the water.

"Oh my God, oh my God." She put her hand to her chest.

It's here, it's here.

They'd been hearing rumors coming out of the Soviet Union of strange creatures, but she'd heard so much bullshit from the communists before, she didn't want to believe it.

President John Winters had interrupted her day with a press conference to address the rumors and say that many of them were real, and the U.S. was actively working to contain the problem.

Hell or not though, Jenny still wanted her vacation, and while the others were starting to panic. . .

She'd been looking up hotels.

The worm shot up from the water and crawled on the beach, looking much like a pitiful beached whale.

The worm lay there for a second before it opened its mouth wide and the bodies of the people it had taken rolled out.

They smacked onto the ground as corpses, their clothes and body shredded from the few seconds in the damn thing's mouth.

But one by one, they started to stand.

And if Jenny had been a little wiser, she would have already been running away.

Instead the people who were once men, widened their dead eyes and were human no longer.

Tentacles burst and wiggled from their flesh and they howled as they ran up the beach and toward the city.

Now, with a scream, Jenny ran.

2 2

MARAT SAT with the team as they overlooked the base. They'd been waiting about an hour or two.

The whole time Marat was entertaining a conversation with himself in his head.

Why the hell did you come back here?

I don't know. Seemed like a reasonable thing at the time.

You know you almost fucking died, right?

Yeah, I didn't forget.

From this patch of ground, Marat could look over and see the barbed wire he'd climbed over. He could even see the patch of woods he did a mad dash through.

At the time, he was so certain he'd never see the place again. He only expected that if returned, it would be because someone dragged him back.

He sat back and sighed. He crossed his legs to get comfortable.

One of the CIA spooks gave him a look, at least Marat thought he did—it was practically impossible to tell what anyone was looking at when they were in CAG—but the operative looked away a few seconds later.

Marat glanced about and noticed everyone was kneeling but he was sitting like a little kid, legs folded together like they were about to go into story time.

He half groaned and leaned up to kneel. It was bad enough he was feeling under dressed after seeing those goddamn aliens—he'd kill for some CAG—but apparently he sat like a little bitch too.

That's right. Everyone here was a hard ass. You could tell that just by the way they wore the CAG. CIA was supposed to be the American spies for all Marat knew, but it seemed Americans even liked their spies to carry around big guns.

They do love their guns.

They were equipped with Soviet CAG and weapons though, so they probably weren't any of the American's first choice in battle.

Still, he took a glance at one operative, a Kate Lee or something from what Marat had heard. When Marat saw her on the base, she looked like she weighed about as much as a wet shoe, but here in CAG, Marat thought she looked just as ready to eat faces as the cronux were.

There was a Darren Walker—or was it Wafer?—too who towered over Marat. He'd stood guard while Marat took a piss back in the woods. Walker held a flame thrower and looked like he just *wished* he'd get a chance to use it.

Marat wasn't even sure why he was thinking about them. Maybe because they were like a mirror showing him all he wasn't.

Another irritation that occurred to him halfway in was that it's not likely that their names were even Kate Lee, Darren Walker, or any of the other names he heard back at the base. They were spies after all.

Marat kept kneeling for a few more minutes while they waited, but his foot started to fall asleep. He took a look around the woods. He was certain there was nothing here, because if there was, it would have already been over here trying to eat them.

Maybe he was just getting pissy because he hadn't had a cigarette, but he decided, *hell with it,* and sat back on his ass and folded his legs.

Walker gave him a look this time. A long, *two* or *three* second look, which was uncomfortably long when a person in CAG with a flamethrower was staring.

I don't care.

Marat shook his head. Here was the truth.

They needed him.

He might not be able to fight worth a damn, and he might not be qualified for CAG, or be comfortable kneeling, but he was the only person here that could turn the gate off if they got in.

"You have to learn to make love to the system. Caress it like a beautiful woman."

That was the voice of his old professor again, and Marat winced as he imagined the man's sickening gestures with his hips.

But it was true.

Marat had to get in there and make love to that system.

Moller turned around and spoke in a hushed whisper. "I'm concerned about those once men down there. They might be sentries, but Winters didn't feel the gate so I'm willing to bet whatever the Phantom nuke did, it's blocking their mental connection. Either way, our primary goal is to disable the gate, or confirm it's inactive."

Kate Lee shook her head. "It's going to be a real bitch if we found out we came all the way here and it's inactive anyway."

"No," Marat said with some defiance. "Gate is still good. I promise. We build it to be strong, but I can break."

"That's the spirit," one of the operatives said and smacked Marat on the arm. "Get in there and break shit."

The smack probably hurt more than the man intended, but Marat appreciated the encouragement. "Thank you," he said in earnest.

Moller asked, "There any way down other than the elevator?"

Marat considered but shook his head. "No. Not after shutdown. We only have elevator."

"That's a real peach," Darren Walker said. "What if the doors open up and that ugly thing is there?"

"Then we kill it, and anything else in our way." Moller said. "Keep your weapons hot until we're clear."

A few minutes later, Moller made the call.

"Let's go."

And the team went out with rifles at the ready. They headed toward the outer fence of the gate, and Marat rushed to keep up. They came to a crouch a few paces from the fence, and Moller waved one of the operatives to the front. He came close with a hand press cutting tool and squeezed the handle, making the scissors on the edge cut down with battery-powered strength. Marat watched as it sliced through the thick fence, and the man trimmed a hole big enough to climb through.

Marat peeked over where he crossed the fence and almost cut his nuts off on barbed wire.

The thought made him shiver.

The operative finished cutting the hole and gave Moller a thumbs up.

She put up two fingers and gestured twice through the hole.

Marat pointed at himself, confused if he was supposed to be doing something, but two operatives got up and darted in. They kept low and kneeled some feet in as they scanned the area with their rifles. A few seconds of silence ticked by and one stuck a finger into the air.

Moller pointed at each of the others and three more went in. Marat pointed at himself again, confused about what he was supposed to be doing, but Moller nodded and grabbed his arm and hurried in.

They passed a half-melted man, who seemed to have outlasted whatever fire was on him. His body was plastered to the grass where it cooled. With a dull awareness, he reached for them as they passed.

There was a woman on the ground seizing, but she had been doing the same the entire time they'd watched.

"*Lift,*" Moller said, and her voice came from the CAG speakers.

They moved as a team toward it and passed by other tortured creatures until they got to the datapad.

One of the operatives, Marat wasn't sure who anymore, moved in close and hit the commands. The lift came up and someone went close and shined his light inside.

There was nothing.

"Clear." He gave a thumbs up.

They all went inside.

"Get us on the right level," Moller said to Marat.

He nodded his head and went to the panel. But half froze. There was a soggy, worm like cronux laying dead right next to the controls, and all the buttons were slick and sticky. Marat glanced back but not one seemed concerned, so he pushed the buttons.

There was a loud *clunk* and the elevator started downward.

They were headed right where he'd come from. Right where this all started.

What were they going to find?

"Gate level," Marat said, with dark inflection.

"Phantom nuke or not, I'm getting fallout readings. You keep your gear on." Moller pointed at Marat.

He nodded and rubbed his thumb and pointer finger together with strings of slime stretching between them.

He sure as hell wasn't taking the suit off.

"Remember, priority one is locating the gate and making it ineffective. Priority two is collecting intelligence." Moller said amongst the team. "But we're heading in deep, so keep your weapons ready." She pointed at an operative. "Get the heavy out."

The operative nodded his heavy CAG helmet and slung his rifle over his shoulder. For a brief moment, Marat wondered if he could even hold the rifle himself, or if it'd tear his arm off when he fired. The operative pulled a rocket propelled grenade launcher off his back and opened the breach to make sure a load was locked in.

"Confirmed," the operative said.

Marat eyeballed the RPG, now that he was *certain* it would rip his arm out of socket.

As the dial on the elevator counted down, Marat felt his breath sharpening.

"Positions," Moller ordered, and the operatives got into formation inside the lift. "Get behind me." She waved to Marat. "These things change constantly. We don't know what we're going to see. Be prepared for anything."

Marat moved to the back of the group and found a discarded container to crouch behind.

The lift rattled when it stopped on the floor. There was a loud engine hum, and the doors slid open.

The team waited, pointing toward the darkness inside, but if they saw something, Marat didn't know. He couldn't see a damn thing from here.

Moller stuck two fingers up and held them for a second before gesturing forward.

"Move out."

They headed out in formation, and Marat slunk behind them.

Orange warning lights spun in the corners of the rooms, but if there had been alarms, they'd long since died.

Each time the light spun, Marat saw blood or bullet casings, but no bodies.

He felt the skin prickle on his back. *"Can't see. . ."* He struggled with each flash of light.

"Keep your hand on my back," Moller said. He reached up and put his hand on her CAG shoulder. "Which way?" she asked.

Marat looked around the entrance room as the orange lights spun. There were blood splatters on the walls and the ground, and he had to wonder how much of it belonged to people he knew.

"Marat, which way?" Moller asked again.

"This way." He pointed.

"You sure?"

"I live here long time. I'm sure."

They started down that way, and the only sounds Marat could hear was his own breathing, the quiet whine of the CAGS near him, and the occasional scratch of metal on metal as he stepped on a bullet casing.

"Here," Marat directed again, and they took another turn, and then another after that.

A few minutes and several hallways and rooms later, Marat pointed forward.

"This to gate."

"The fuck is that?" one operative said.

Marat frowned, he didn't know what the man was talking about.

"*It's moving,*" someone else said.

"What?" Marat asked.

As the light flashed, Marat caught only a glance at what they were talking about.

A bubbling, dark purple flesh moving on the ground.

"I can't see!" Marat said and took a step back.

The light flashed again and tentacles speared out of the flesh and hit one of the operatives. "Fuck!" the man yelled and was quickly pulled in.

"Torch it!" Moller ordered.

A blast of flame went roaring past Marat and hit the flesh.

There was a large center lump that squirmed.

Marat cursed in Ukrainian and stumbled back.

The operative was squirming beneath it.

Another blast of flame illuminated the room and a dozen mouths opened on the flesh, all screaming.

There was a roar and Marat looked up.

The light spun in the distance and went over top of the large, hulking beast dragging its thick tail.

Its large, malformed eyes crawled with yellow veins, and it focused on them.

"Shoot it!" Moller ordered, and there were flashes of light as the guns went off.

Marat winced and put his hands on his ears. The sound was almost deafening inside the hallways.

He could see now as Walker burst another flame onto the screaming flesh. The lump in the center was shifting toward the gate room, and the rifle fire illuminated the hulking beast charging their way.

It opened its mouth and had thick, fist-sized teeth inside its beak of a mouth.

Marat's will snapped.

He wasn't brave in the best of circumstances.

And as the team engaged enemies on two fronts, this was hardly the best of circumstances. Marat knew this was coming. He expected a fight.

He expected to die.

But *knowing* he'd die and standing to greet it were two very different things.

Marat moved as the flashes of rifles lit up the area and the squad called out orders.

He went in the other direction, stumbling at first and then running.

But oh, Marat, he'd promised himself no more running, hadn't he?

Those promises were easier to make in an air conditioned room and harder to keep when confused and blind.

An emergency light flashed overhead, and Marat nearly came face to face with the same fleshy patch that swallowed the man. It had grown over the wall here.

Three golf-ball-sized lumps on different patches opened into eyeballs and glared at him.

Marat squinted and saw a mouth the size of a man opened with a wet howl that strangely reminded Marat of the times when they would feed his elderly, toothless grandmother.

Another blast of flame from down the hallway illuminated things more clearly, with Marat's shadow cast onto the wall flesh.

Tentacles came off the wall with startling speed, and Marat went backward and tripped. The tentacles slapped down toward him but he pulled his feet out of the way and they only left a wet smear on the floor.

When he came up, he saw Darren Walker down the hall shooting a flamethrower at something Marat couldn't see. The flame illuminated the area and monstrous screams from a dozen voices filled the air.

He shot a glance back and saw the tentacles from the wall quivering as they stretched farther, and the wet mouth in the center made gulping motions.

Marat hopped to his feet and took off in another direction.

With no real purpose or direction, he went away from the fight and away from the terror on the wall. Spinning emergency lights offered only faint illumination, and in his panic he lost track of where he was. As the light died and the hallway went dark again, he slammed into a wall this time, but thankfully, the wall didn't attempt to eat him. Instead he fell on his ass and saw the blood patterns everywhere.

He got to his feet again and heard Moller scream.

"Bring it down!"

Moller.

He'd left her behind.

Marat, the cowardly fool, hadn't just run for his life, he'd abandoned his team.

Refocused, he stomped a foot. "Shit!" he said in Ukrainian.

He came all the way here just to run at the first sign of trouble?

"Get together dumb turd shit," he said in broken English.

What could he do?

He put a hand on the wall and idly glanced back and forth as he considered.

There was only one thing he could do.

Turn off the gate.

Moller's voice rang in his mind.

"Priority one is locating the gate and making it ineffective."

There was no way to go the way they were going, so he'd have to go another. But he knew this place like the back of his hand and could get into the gate room another way.

Marat moved quickly.

To say things weren't going as planned would be an understatement, but then again, who could have planned for crawling, aggressive flesh?

"Torch it!"

Moller ordered and the flame shot out, and the flesh screamed with a dozen voices.

But then the other creature, the hulking beast, made its way toward them.

The operatives were already moving to position, and Moller had seconds to form a plan.

The alternatives clicked in her head.

Head back to the elevator and possibly be trapped as the creature moved in?

Rush toward the gate room and form a perimeter despite unknown, hostile entity crawling on the floor and walls?

Take a chance and choose another hallway and potentially meet some other unknown entity.

The choices were thin.

She made the best decision she could.

Stand and fight.

"Shoot it!"

She aimed her own rifle and fired shots at the oncoming hulk. Her CAG helmet balanced out the flashes of blinding light and rifle fire. She saw every shot hit as her team formed and fired.

But the bullets smacked into the creature's thick hide with no real concern.

"It's still got him!" Darren Walker said as he continued with the flamethrower on the flesh. "It pulled him into the gate room." He let out another burst of flame.

"Cook it," she called to him and then pointed at the soldier with the RPG. "Heavy, up front."

The operative came around and knelt down as he put the RPG on his shoulder and fired. The grenade screamed through the air and slammed into the hulk, blowing its entire left arm off and throwing wet meat against the wall.

The hulk spun from the hit and crashed into the wall, but came back up on its feet seconds later.

Moller looked over her shoulder again as Darren Walker blasted fire farther down the hallway. He was standing on the cooked flesh and it cracked beneath her foot.

Priority one.

Bring down the gate.

"Cover, cover! This way," she called out as she kept firing and retreated toward the gate room.

———

A LIGHT FLASHED and rolled away. Marat put his hand on the wall and used it to guide himself in.

With deep, careful breaths, he steadied his focus and moved toward the gate room.

The hallway went dark and he continued with a slow walk.

As the light flashed by again, a large eye the size of a dinner plate opened on the wall and looked at him.

Startled, Marat punched it and felt the center shift beneath his knuckles. The eye shut tight and Marat pulled off the wall.

The light flashed again and he saw that the flesh was growing down the wall and part of the floor was uncovered.

Throwing caution to the wind, Marat ran toward the gate room.

A green glow cast out of the room and Marat ran toward it. The bubbling, creeping flesh had crawled over much of the walls and floor, but there were still bare patches.

In the center of the room was the green, glowing gate, and the flesh was growing out of it. Marat pressed his back to the bare wall as he saw eyes of all sizes open up inside the room and stare at him.

The consoles were still lit up and glowing, though the flesh had grown over some.

With green light cast over him, Marat dashed over to the energy console.

He took a seat at it and scooted closer.

A thin vine of reaching flesh grew up from the cracks of a console button, apparently having already taken root inside the internals of the machines.

The tiny vine pointed toward Marat. Wincing hard, Marat glanced around and found an empty cup. He turned it over and sat it on top of the vine as he focused.

Something growled behind him, and Marat shifted his weight, and practically already felt the teeth digging into his neck.

A massive saggy flesh being was hanging out of the gate, like it was a friendly neighbor sticking its head in through an open window.

Fat, wrinkled fingers gripped either side of the gate, and its face looked like piles of skin melted together. And as if there were a sudden jerk, the skin pulled back and it formed a human face. Its mouth sagged open and it growled once more.

Marat turned back to the console just as slowly as he turned away from it, the whole time taking the thought of the creature behind him and mentally setting it aside so he could focus.

He tapped at the keys.

MOLLER WAS GOING TO DIE—SO was her team.

"Keep moving!" she called out as Darren Walker blasted fire to kill the flesh and lead them in.

This whole place reminded her of Felicity; she even had the same crawling dread under her skin. They'd lost Marat already, he must have gotten lost in the confusion or moved to take cover—but with him, so went their chance of disabling the gate.

Her only choice was to blow it up now.

The hulk barreled into the main hallway as their heavy finished loading the RPG.

"*Blast it*," Moller ordered and the man took a knee again.

The grenade shot through the air and hit the beast again. It opened a powerful wound on its chest, but the creature was only momentarily slowed.

Roaring open its beak-like mouth and displaying its teeth, the creature took off in a barreling run.

There was no more time.

"Move," Moller ordered the team back and they dashed over the still living flesh.

They were going to die, and she was okay with that so long as she brought the gate down.

They entered into the room, and the green glow of the gate bathed them with light. But only a few steps into the room, the flesh beneath them opened up and Kate Lee was sucked into a wide mouth.

Darren Walker surged heat over it, and blasted it across the rest of their feet.

The mouth fell away and left Kate as the fire climbed up their legs. Inside the CAG they couldn't feel the heat, and Moller screamed, "Burn it all."

Darren Walker let loose with the flame, as Moller scanned the room.

She saw the gate—something was hanging out of it.

A horrible creature that looked like pancake batter as it was poured onto a skillet, but it had a face. . .

It was the face of Cameron Elliot, her boyfriend that died on Felicity.

Moller froze in place.

The being leaned farther out of the gate and stretched its arm toward her.

———

MARAT IGNORED ALL ELSE, even the rattle of gunfire and screams as they erupted behind him. He was too busy.

He was making love to the system.

Oddly, he remembered the cooing face of his professor as he made gentle hip thrusts, and Marat had the same sickened look on his face, but it helped him focus.

He'd been useless so far, but this was his element. The Soviets had recognized his talent and drew him from university before he was ever finished, and they placed him in one of their most discreet programs they had.

Lines of code strung across the screen, and Marat kept gentle taps on the keys as he input new commands and bypassed security guards.

He was never going to be the man with the gun, or the hardass in CAG.

But he could still feel like Superman.

A Superman who smoked, had synthetic lungs, and made love to computers.

He turned toward the gate and saw the skin sack horror hanging amidst the glowing light and reaching toward Moller.

"Eat shit fat beef," Marat said with the deepest growl he could manage.

He pressed the command key.

IT HAD ALMOST BEEN like a spell over her, seeing Elliot's face, but it all ended suddenly.

"Eat shit fat beef," Marat said from across the room, but Moller had no idea what that meant.

The gate flashed brightly and then cut along with all the console lights in the room.

Cut in mid-air, the reaching arms and Elliot's head dropped to the floor. They smashed into the ground and popped like water balloons filled with black tar.

Moller had only a moment to think before the hulk barreled in behind them.

The crawling flesh on the floor and walls opened with hundreds of tiny mouths that all screamed with dying breath.

The hulk snatched up Darren Walker and flames kept shooting from his weapon as the hulk squeezed him in his grip. The CAG crushed in like a soda can and Walker hadn't even the time to scream.

The operative with the RPG aimed, but the hulk threw Walker's body and it smashed into him.

Those two went scattering across the floor while the last two operatives fired.

Bullet casings flashed out from their rifles, and some rounds smashed into the computer screens and made flashes of sparks surge up.

Fire ripped around by their legs as they continued to fight.

The hulk barreled forward with a furious roar, careless of the flames as it came for Moller.

She let out a breath and picked her shot as she squeezed the target.

The round blew through its large eye and the creature reared up with its hand on its face.

Kate Lee dashed forward and picked up the dropped RPG and aimed it at the creature's exposed midsection.

Thunk.

The explosion hit it right in the center and hurled wet meat away.

The creature collapsed to a knee but pulled its head up with a wet sneer.

Moller and the last two standing operatives aimed their rifles and let loose a barrage on its face.

Rounds dug at its face until its flesh gave way and the bone started to break. The creature tried to lift up its arm, but it was too wounded and only succeeded in falling flat.

Moller closed in as she released her magazine and fed in another.

She let loose another barrage that pulped its head and made the dying body jitter.

Moller stood still for a moment, still carefully aiming as the end of her rifle smoked.

With a few seconds of silence, she spoke.

"Davis, go see if Perez is still alive, and Lee," Moller said as she leaned up, content the creature was dead. "Go take out all the hard drives."

Marat leaned up from the console with a confused look. "Hard drives?"

"Priority two," Moller said as Marat's eyes widened. "Secure all Soviet intelligence."

"What about priority three?" Kate Lee asked.

Marat looked between them. "What's priority three?"

Moller paused to look Marat in the eyes. He was confused and didn't understand.

It didn't matter.

"Secure live parasites. We'll get those from the infected outside."

McAndrews reached to the center of the table and pressed the button that ended the conference call. The small green light on the console phone turned off.

John sat in silence with Roles and McAndrews as they contemplated what they heard.

French Prime Minister and European Federation Chairman Moshe Sarrazin had just given them a report.

There were new outbreaks in Italy, France, and West Germany.

John rubbed his chin and stared at the conference phone.

McAndrews broke the silence. "So much for that whole idea of containing things in the Soviet Union."

Roles cleared his throat. "With those three European nations and the Soviet Union, we can also add outbreaks in Iran and China. I'd be unwilling to discount the idea that we're aware of all outbreaks. If they are as far inland as France, then I have to believe there are more outbreaks we're yet to be made aware of."

"Thanks." McAndrews nodded his head. "You always know how to add a little spice to a shit sandwich."

John spoke, his voice rough from lack of sleep. "He's right. We need to know where we stand. What's the situation in China?"

"Indeterminable." Roles's voice was clear and calm. "My sources aren't able to obtain concrete information."

"Who the hell are these sources you're always touting? How the hell do we know who we can even trust?" McAndrews made a face as he rolled up his sleeves.

Roles gave him a flat look and said nothing.

"Roles might be a bastard, but he hasn't been wrong," John interjected.

"Oh, he's certainly my favorite bastard." McAndrews snorted. "What are we going to do for the Europeans? Are you going to give them what they requested?"

"Military aid?" John asked. "Where do you suppose I dig it up? Our active personnel are all engaged."

"So we tell them to eat shit?" McAndrews made a face. "Seems a bit odd to supply the Soviets and give them air cover but leave the Europeans in the dark."

"*No,*" John insisted. "I wasn't saying that. It was an honest question." He looked at Roles. "Where the hell can we transfer troops from?"

"I could come up with some places." Roles sat back in his chair. "We have most of our Euro command forces in Greece, but if we move them around, Turkey might start trying its luck again. Those two hate each other."

"You think Turkey would try and kick things up again even with an alien outbreak? Aren't we in an alliance?"

"A little ink and a lot of paper say they're in an alliance, sure." Roles nodded. "But they've been bickering for a few thousand years, so I don't see an alien invasion quite stopping that."

John exhaled loudly. "We'll shift our forces there and provide aerial support."

McAndrews spoke, "What about the Soviets? The Europeans are already disengaging their aircraft from supporting the Soviets. If we do too, then they're going to lose a lot of their advantage."

"The Soviets are stabilized, and with their automated aerial defenses, we can't do anything for them that far inland without risk of being shot down. And from what I've heard, my daughter has given them room to breathe. That correct, Roles?"

"Yes, sir. They've just secured Warsaw and are in the process of landing liberating Soviet aircraft there."

"Then how about we move her to the European Federation?" McAndrews asked. "Start stomping out some of these fires before they blaze?"

John could practically feel a growl roll up his throat.

Move his daughter there?

Was she a piece of equipment?

Was she supposed to stay on the front lines until she died?

"I'm sure the Europeans expect us to," Roles said. "If she stays active in the Soviet Union while they have their own outbreaks, then there will be some definite breaks in our relationship."

"Either way, now is the time to twist a few arms with the debt negotiation." McAndrews tapped his knuckles on the table.

John rubbed his brow and shook his head. "Why the hell do you always go there?"

"Go where? You mean make decisions for the country? I think moving some fighter craft there and a few thousand soldiers is more than enough of a good reason to put a delay on some of that compounding interest. Perhaps an indefinite delay with a few new economic market openings. You act like we didn't just do the same thing to the Soviets."

John rubbed his brow again again. He had a tension headache wrapping around his brain. He grabbed a glass of water from the center of the table and took a drink.

McAndrews wasn't wrong. Most good deals were made when the other side was bent over the table.

The U.S. had finagled several powerful international institutions into moving across the Atlantic in exchange for entering World War I on the Allies' side.

John had read Woodrow Wilson's entry about it in the Book of Secrets yesterday.

"A man at sea can view the beach from a distance, but he only sees a solid

brick of yellow. It's only the man with his feet on the ground that can see every grain of sand."

That was a line from the passage. It meant that it was easy to judge the situation and make the *correct* call from a distance, but it was much harder when in the middle of the issue and knew each individual problem.

Have to get a bone for Congress if you want their approval and support.

John took in a deep breath. "We'll discuss it later. I'm concerned about China."

"Why are we so concerned about China?" McAndrews lifted his hands. "We have to be concerned about ourselves and our European allies. Let China handle China."

John gave a dull look to McAndrews. "China shares a border with India and Pakistan, and it's a hop, skip, and a jump from Indonesia. Those four countries together account for half of the world's population, so yes, I'm concerned."

"I see the point, but if we spend our time more concerned with the Chinese and the Soviets over the Europeans, then we're going to find ourselves up shit's creek when we need help."

John exhaled deeply; he was getting tired. "McAndrews, I don't say this often, and it might be due to the collapse of the world or my lack of sleep, but you're starting to piss me off. I'm not talking about taking our eyes off the Europeans. I'm saying we just understand where the threat priorities are."

McAndrews scoffed and held up his hands as if in defeat. "All right, you said it. I'll contact our ambassadors and relay the message that we'd like to help the nations bordering China to prepare their defenses, but if you want to do anything for China, you're going to have to make contact with them yourself."

"I get it." John nodded.

"One more thing." Roles held up a finger. "I've had reports that the Chinese have developed their own *Ghost*."

"Ghost? You mean like Alice?" John raised an eyebrow.

Roles nodded. "They call the program Dragonskin. As far as I'm aware, they have only one, but I believe they're ramping up to make more."

"How are they doing that?"

"Controlled infections."

"*God.*" John shook his head. "They're infecting people on purpose? And they successfully produced one?"

"Yes, but he's not Han Chinese, he's a Kasher."

John raised his eyebrows. "What did they do, pull him out of a labor camp?"

"Yes," Roles said with a flat inflection. "I can't believe that would be their first choice, so the process to change someone must be incredibly difficult or costly. They haven't made any announcements though. Possibly the whole Kasher situation has been sensitive after the sanctions we placed on them for the camps. The Chinese still deny they exist."

"I'm sure. Keep me updated on *Dragonskin*. Until then. . ." John considered and nodded his head. "We'll move those troops out of Greece. I want you to find anymore we can spare. Contact Euro Command and tell them to develop deployment and containment plans." He looked to McAndrews. "You make contact with the South East Asian alliance ambassadors and see where we can provide support or coordination. We can't afford to sit idly by if things spill out of China and into India."

McAndrews gave an exhausted shake of his head. "I'm telling you we need to tread carefully. The Chinese won't take kindly to any kind of military build up on their borders. They don't trust us not to take advantage of them. We might end up distracting them and forcing them to move troops to the border themselves."

"If the Chinese think I'm about to march in and take a bite out of them while things are spreading across Europe, then we're doomed as a race. But I understand the concerns. I'll request to have contact with Chairman Zhao."

The door opened and a young aide stuck her head in, "Sir!"

The three men turned around to look at her with concerned faces.

"There's been an outbreak in New York."

MILES HADN'T LIKED IT, but he and Kevin had personally gone down the line of each man in their convoy and inspected their genitals while a hard-faced mother of four that looked like she could eat nails checked all the women.

Miles recalled the mother chewing on a cigar while a babe still nursed on her breast as Endo explained the game plan to the leaders of the group.

She pulled the cigar out of her mouth and showed her yellow teeth just as the baby pulled off her breast. Miles couldn't pull his eyes away as she took the time to stuff the cigar into her mouth and reposition the baby before she bothered to cover herself.

Kevin had remarked that it didn't seem right to ask a nursing woman to do the work.

"Ask her? She self appointed herself the leader of the women. Any woman who tucks her cigar back into her mouth before hiding her tit isn't someone you say no to."

After everyone was inspected, Miles gave a thumbs up to Endo.
"Clear."

After that, he volunteered for another turn behind the wheel and Kevin offered to sit in front with him.

Endo had some reluctance about giving it up, but they passed a military patrol a few miles back that told them they were in the safe zone and needed to keep heading to Berlin.

"It's smooth sailing from here on out, just go take a break, mate."

Endo agreed and went back to eat a few things the newcomers had provided.

An hour into the drive, and Miles was starting to regret ever volunteering. He had to keep pulling at the crotch of his pants. He found a pair of mass produced Soviet pants back at the town, and it was like the bastard communist hated blue jeans so much that they wanted to do the exact opposite of that.

His pants were a dull brown and rode high in the crotch.

He pulled at the pants again and adjusted himself.

"The hell do you think these communist bastards are doing making pants your dick doesn't sit right in?" Miles was behind the wheel again and Kevin was sitting up front. "It's like they expect you to tuck it up into your waistband."

Kevin shrugged and scribbled in a notebook.

"Seriously, they have the best functioning rail system in the world, but they haven't figured out how to master the seam of a pair of pants."

"Guess not," Kevin said and scribbled more.

Still holding the wheel, Miles flashed Kevin a look. "Mate, look ahead. That's Berlin right there. We're almost in the safe and clear."

Kevin glanced up and grinned, then he went back down into his book.

"You never cease to amaze me." Miles shook his head. "What are you writing that's so important there? *Dear Diary, I saw Miles West-wood's wanker. Highlight of my week.*"

"I'm writing down everything we saw and know about the—uhh." He flittered his hands. "The clone things."

"Really?"

"Yeah." He tapped his head. "While it's all fresh. I'm going to give it to the commanders there."

"Mate, this is the goddamn Soviet military, not to mention their intelligence services. I'm certain that whatever pitiful little details we've come to learn, they already know that and more."

"Maybe. Maybe not." Kevin kept scribbling.

"Why's it taking you so long? How hard is it to write—*they don't have dicks?*"

"I'm writing everything we've seen, how they reacted, what they looked like and I'm writing multiple copies."

"What, you don't think they have a photocopy machine there, mate?"

"Just doing my part."

Miles snorted, but it actually gave him a tinge of guilt.

He'd been wondering if Berlin would offer a stiff drink and a warm shower. He hadn't at all thought what he could provide.

"You know what?" Miles kept his eyes on the road. "You're all right, kid."

Kevin put his pen down on his notebook. "Actually, I've been wanting to tell you. Thank you for saving me."

"What?" Kevin's tone caught Miles off guard. "You think I was just going to watch your bits get chewed off? It'd sour my mood."

"No." Kevin shook his head. "You jumped into it. I know what kinda risk you were taking."

"Ahh, don't mention it, mate. You've saved my ass, I owed you."

"No." Kevin shook his head again. "When you did that, I got a flash back to Westwood's Wild World seasons one and two. I've watched them a hundred times. I remember that look in your eye when you met that lady saying she was talking to her dead husband. I remember you giving her a hug. That wasn't faked, that was who you were."

Miles chuckled under his breath. "The hell is this? You doing another psyche evaluation of me? Cut it out."

"I didn't realize it before, but in the later seasons, you got jaded and lost that compassion."

"*Fuck me, mate, just—*"

"It became about the money. You said it. But that's not who you are. You're that guy that hugs widows."

"Mate." Miles's tone flattened. "I'm the guy that hugs widows and puts it on TV for money."

"No, that was a candid shot that got leaked. I heard the conversation where you told her about God and how she'd see her husband again. You said she needed to get the hell away from the men taking her money and lying to her about her husband."

"Someone, uhh, caught that on video?" Miles glanced at Kevin.

"It was on the message boards. It wasn't widely shared. They got it off the woman's own security camera. That's who you were when the camera wasn't rolling."

Miles still chuckled and shook his head as he tried to find the right words while his eyes got wet.

"That other guy? The one who talks about women and booze? That's not Miles Westwood. That's the character."

"Come here." With one hand on the wheel, Miles reached out with the other and put it around Kevin's head. He tugged him closer. "Get over here, you little shit, give 'ems a kiss." He puckered his lips.

"Get off me! Get off!" Kevin wrestled from his grip.

"You think you can sweet talk me like all that and not get at least a little tongue? *Come here.*" The truck shifted, and Miles pulled back with a wince. He shook a finger at Kevin. "All right, no kiss, but I'm buying you a drink and all as soon as we're away from the commies."

ENDO SPENT the last few hours on the road to Berlin in the back. He wasn't sure why he agreed. He hadn't ridden back there the entire time, but he supposed he wanted to.

The truck had gone silent when he climbed in with them. He supposed it might still be hard for some of them to see a South Japanese in CAG when their countries had been enemies for so long.

He popped his CAG helmet and it puffed air as he took it off. He could feel the bristles on his chin—certainly not regulation—but he supposed he had to make some exceptions.

He set the helmet down alongside him as the truck started and he opened his pouch to get the few bits of food he had—a fruit paste and a sticky apple juice that when mixed together for the right consistency, might do the trick to settle the snake in his gut.

Just at that thought, it slithered inside him and he paused for a moment and waited for the pain to pass.

"Here," an elderly woman said and moved to take a seat next to him. "Let me do it."

"No, it's fine."

The elderly woman brushed that aside and took the food out of his hands. Despite the truck moving, she carefully squeezed the fruit pace into the juice.

"You speak Russian very well," a man further down the truck said. "You have a central accent. Sounds like you were born in Moscow."

"Thank you." Endo tipped his head with respect.

The elderly woman grinned and handed the mix back to him.

Endo smiled back as he took it, but even that felt awkward and strange on his face.

"Where are you from?" a young man with a lame leg asked.

"South Japan."

"What kind of food do you eat there?" a teenaged girl asked.

Endo had just opened his mouth when the elderly woman waved them all away.

"Let him eat first, poor boy is half starved. Look how thin those cheeks are." She put her hand under Endo's wrist and gestured it up.

With another grin he tipped his head back and squeezed the mix into his mouth.

When he looked back he saw everyone in the truck was looking at him and ready to ask him a question, but a young blonde Russian woman leaned her elbow onto her knees and asked him a question.

"So are you married?"

———

ENDO STEPPED off the truck with his helmet in hand, and for the first time in days, his stomach pain had dulled to a bearable level, which was fortunate as he just experienced one of the most awkward moments of his life.

There were times throughout his life when he'd had casual conversations, but it was always with the boys he grew up with in Three Raven, and never with civilians, and certainly not with non-Japanese.

But despite how strange it all was, it wasn't bad. It was nice to see people's faces and hear their voices.

Endo felt a certain kind of peace to it all.

He looked over to see Miles and Kevin talking with Rat. Endo took the moment to look around Berlin. Despite the chaos of refugees and trucks entering, it was still a beautiful city.

Miles and Kevin walked his way, both calling out and waving to Rat who waved back and gave an exaggerated bow before heading off with most of the others from the truck.

"Well, mate, the entrance guards told us all foreigners have to go check in with the station chief, but I don't see any reasons why we couldn't all just bugger off if we wanted. They seem too occupied to care much for us. Get us a car, and we could make it to the border in no time." Miles shrugged his shoulders. "What'd ya think?"

"If that is your way, I'll wish you luck, but I mean to turn myself into the station chief as directed."

Miles frowned. "All right, but what after that?"

"South Japanese forces will be sent to retrieve me and I'll be taken into custody."

Kevin made a face like he heard a bad joke. "What? Why the hell would you want to do that?"

"Kota, listen mate, we've got plenty of options beyond imprisonment. Come with me. Nice-looking fellow like yourself will be popular with the ladies. It'll change that whole rotten attitude right away."

"Thank you, but no." Endo nodded.

"That's it then?" Kevin shrugged and glanced between Miles and Endo.

"Suppose so." Miles frowned at Endo. "I'm not going to let you take the walk alone, I'll go with you."

Kevin nodded. "Might as well." He patted his bag. "I want to hand these off anyway."

Endo cast one glance back to the truck and saw the grandfather who first pleaded with Endo for mercy pulled his hat off and held it over his chest as he nodded at Endo.

Endo nodded back.

It made him feel warm, but it didn't matter.

Soon he was going to be sent back to Japan and face the consequences of his desertion.

Public execution.

If there was a time to evade that fate, then it was now, within the chaos of the collapse of the Soviet Union.

It would be an easy thing for him to slip off and never be seen again, he certainly had the skills for it.

But no.

Endo, despite the snake in his stomach and the exhaustion in his eyes, had never felt more full and complete.

Were those people from the truck enough to undo the horrors of his life? All the men he'd killed just like that grandfather?

That answer was of course, no.

He would face the consequences of his decisions, and he would accept his punishments.

It was the will of Heaven.

25

ALICE STEPPED off the ship in the hangar bay and her support team came onto her like a pit crew in a car race.

She'd just finished a mission, but she had an odd, sinking feeling in her stomach.

It felt like the moment of blindness that comes after the lights are flipped on.

Her mind was crawling, and so much of it was happening at once, that it was hard to know what was happening at all.

One of the crew members reached for her rifle and she handed it over, though in all honesty, she rarely shot it these days.

She stood in place as they used their armory tools and took off the pieces of her CAG and fit them into a soft casing for repair and maintenance.

Stripped down to the black skin suit beneath the armor, one of the crew men motioned for her to take a seat and pull the suit up on her arm with the synthetic hand.

With a dull nod, Alice sat down and adjusted the sleeve, careful not to damage any of the circuitry embedded within.

"How's it working?" the crewman asked as he repositioned the arm to her side for a better view.

Not bothering to make eye contact, Alice answered, "There are some malfunctions in the precision of the fingers."

"Did it get a bad bump?"

"Possibly. It's war."

"No kidding," the man said and rubbed his thumb over the edge of her wrist. The lip of her synthetic skin pulled up and the crewman grabbed a tool to lift the flesh.

Her black synthetic skin weave peeled up and exposed the bone-like machinery beneath. Alice gave it a casual glance and looked away.

"Processors and firing joints look jammed. Give me a second." He reached for another tool.

"Sure."

The man leaned in close as he started to adjust her hand. "You know, I don't just work on these, I'm also a counselor for people with synthetic limbs. There's a psychological aspect to how these things work."

"That so?" Alice asked, still not bothering to look.

"Yep." He adjusted something. "How's that feel?" He placed the back of his hand in Alice's grip.

She carefully squeezed his hand and the sensors and processors sent indications wired into her nerves. She could feel his warm hand.

"Like it's real." She looked over at him as he worked now. "But the fingers are a little numb."

"Got it." He kept speaking as he worked, "You see, it's not just in the limb itself. Get things wrong here." He tapped his head. "And it'll keep going off."

"What are you saying exactly?" She only noticed then that the man was about her father's age, and reminded her of him some too. Though the man had grayer hair.

He shrugged. "No offense, of course. It's common among veterans. Less so in the civilian population, but it happens there too. I've treated both." He reached for another tool that looked like a small set of pliers and used them to reach into her hand to adjust a small band. "There we go. Now how's that?" He set his hand back in hers again.

She gripped his hand and he smiled back at her.

"Feels like the real thing."

He patted her arm and squeezed her hand back. "It doesn't *feel* like it. It is. This *is* your hand, Ms. Winters. We might have to make the occasional adjustment, but just because we need a little help doesn't mean it's not real."

Alice watched him for a second and nodded.

"I appreciate it," she said.

"That's what I'm here for." He flattened the skin back down on her arm and put his tools away as he spoke. "I know you're a busy lady, but you want a recommendation?"

"You're the expert." She gave him a soft grin. "Let me hear it."

"You're going to keep having problems with this if you don't take a breather. I can appreciate the circumstances you're under, but you need the occasional break from your thoughts. Call your son. I know it's hard to do, but you've got to slow down and get the occasional reminder that you're human or you're going to wear yourself out." He pointed at her arm. "This we can replace, but *this*." He tapped his head again. "I don't have the right tools for."

Alice took in a deep breath and exhaled.

"I might just do that."

"Hey, it's the best medicine." He reached down and pulled up his pant leg, revealing an entire synthetic leg. He winked at her. "I know."

ALICE WAS CONFLICTED.

The odd sensation inside her that made her feel off balance and uneven was like a hole she kept digging at. The deeper she went, the further she got from reality.

The man was right, she needed to call her son and get back in touch with what was important.

She grinned as she stepped toward the door to her private room.

What was the man's name? She didn't know, but she'd be sure to ask next time she saw him. In fact, come to think of it, she barely knew anyone on the base. Either the Soviets that fought with her or the team that took care of her, she hardly even looked them in the face.

Her door opened and she stepped inside. She peeled off the jacket she'd picked up from the crew and tossed it over a chair.

The man was right. She was losing her mind and it was all because she let things get too deep and stepped further and further away from who she was.

She looked at the time and saw that it'd be around midday for Eli.

He might even be having lunch.

Alice grabbed a protein bar and peeled it open. She took a bite and another deep breath as she picked up the phone.

She dialed Cora's number and put it to her ear.

She loved Eli—she *wanted* to talk to him—so she didn't know why it was so hard.

The phone rang once.

Twice.

Cora picked up on the third ring.

"Cora, it's—"

"Alice? Oh my God, Alice."

"What's wrong?"

"Did you see it? The TV just put it on right now. Those poor people."

"Cora, what are you talking about? Slow down."

"It's here Alice, it's here."

The conversation only went for a few more minutes as Cora panicked and told her what was happening.

There was a swirl of panic in Alice's chest after she hung up the phone.

She loudly gasped and put her hands in her hair.

She'd seen what the cronux could do. She knew how they laid waste to cities.

New York.

Her home was in New York.

Flashes of long limbed monsters breaking down doors and dragging screaming people from their homes flashed through her mind.

There had been a way to disconnect when it was a people that weren't hers that spoke a language she didn't understand.

But this would be her neighbors.

Her country.

Her family.

From what Cora told Alice, it just started happening. Alice could be the only one on base who knew it yet.

Holding her hair and pacing as she took loud gasps of air, she knew how this happened.

The Janissary had sucked her in.

Arrogant, distracted, and hungry to kill, she hadn't been careful. She hadn't been looking closely when they moved past her.

And now they were in her home.

What could she do? What could she do?

She stopped suddenly, her hands still tight in her hair.

I have to find them. I have to stop them now.

Alice let go of her hair.

She took a step to the mirror and leaned down, placing her palms flat in front of it.

She stared into her own eyes.

They were human eyes.

She was human.

She couldn't forget.

She was going to go deeper into the hive mind than she'd ever been.

Alice found a spot in the center of her room and went down onto her ass. She folded her legs beneath her and placed her hands on her knees.

She thought of Eli, she thought of Cora, and she thought of her father.

With her mind clear and focused, she knew there wasn't a thing in the world she wouldn't do for the people she loved.

Alice leaned her head back and closed her eyes.

She took a deep breath.

A darkness flowed upon her as she sank into a pit.

A void was there in the center that swallowed all that neared it, even the darkness.

She went to the center and slipped into the void.

IF ALICE HAD legs in this world, then she was walking within a marsh that flowed up to her knees. And if this world was real, which it wasn't, then she had a candle in hand with only a faint light.

At the edges of the light, she could see things stir and move—bony tails and rigid, hissing jaws.

She wasn't here for them.

Each step she took was hard, and the ground sucked at her feet.

She wasn't supposed to be here.

This place wasn't meant for her.

No good thing ever came here.

No good thing ever left.

She needed to find him, but the madness within had grown and it screamed with a thousand voices. How could she hear one voice from any other? How could she find them?

If the Archon screamed here in the darkness—this place that wasn't real and she had no right to—then his voice would be loudest of all, for he was the prince of this false world.

King of the void.

God of the becoming.

She found strands pulsing on the ground like veins, but there were too many. and when she looked back—the place where she'd entered —the light had softened and the darkness had closed in.

Could she ever find her way back?

She wouldn't know, not before she found him.

There wasn't a thing in this world or any other she wouldn't do for the people she loved.

The veins pulsed with the blood. Alice picked upon and pinched it until it tore.

The blood flowed upon the ground.

She looked upon the surrounding darkness once more.

She would not find the Archon.

Perhaps he would find her.

Alice hated them.

They had taken much from her, and she too felt the madness.

She screamed and joined her voice to theirs.

Her hate was strong, and it was loud. It thundered through the hive mind, and if the Archon was king, then his voice was loudest of all.

But she challenged him.

And he heard the call.

Before her, the darkness pulled away like a parting curtain.

She saw the Archon.

A powerful standing beast, with bubbles moving beneath his skin.

Ever changing. Ever growing.

He stood tall, nude but sexless, and he had powerful wings that spread behind him.

A circle of followers crowded near him.

She met him in this world, but to kill him. . .

She would need to find him in the other.

How could she do it? How, though all the noise and madness, could she take him and find the veins in the real world that led to him?

A voice—the Archon—spoke to her, for her thoughts were loud and known to all.

You but only need ask. . .

WHEN ALICE CAME out of the trance, she moved again to the mirror.

"You are human," she said, even if the words were hard to believe. "And you kill monsters."

After that, she put her jacket back on and went to find Grand Marshal Garin in the officer's quarters.

Garin was stone faced when she walked in, a gray haired man with dark eyes and synthetic jaw that gave him troubles.

"I suppose you've heard the news?" His accented voice was a tired strain.

"New York, and outbreaks in Italy, France, and West Germany."

"And more." Garin shook his head. "We haven't heard from the U.S. yet, but they'll want you on the first plane possible. You need to go gather your things."

"No. We need to get a strike team together."

Garin's eyes narrowed. "What's your plan?"

"I'm going to end it here. I'm going to kill him."

THE ARCHON HAD BEEN high in the air when he felt the woman enter into his mind.

He'd called for her before; he invited her in.

She never came.

She was here now.

And she wanted him.

A heat came from her that made the void recede, a beauty that came from a being that walked in both worlds.

She was beautiful in all ways.

He could have kept her.

This was his world, and she was foolish to have entered.

Upon his will, he could have reached out and warped her mind.

Remade her.

But then he would only have her mind.

He wanted her body, he wanted her whole.

There, within the hive mind, no words were exchanged, but only ever an understanding.

She would be allowed to leave.

And she would come to him.

He told her where he was, and where he would be.

The horde was beneath him, but even now, it broke into pieces and scattered to attack other lands. The largest still followed him directly and they swept the land and picked it clean.

They followed him as a King.

They loved him as a god.

But they would have to wait.

He dove faster and picked up speed, leaving the horde behind.

When he met the woman. . .

He would do so alone.

"He'll be alone," Alice told the Grand Marshal.

"How do you know?" he asked.

"He promised."

With that said, Garin declared that they would throw everything they had at the Archon.

It took forty five minutes to refuel and scramble the jets and drop-ships, suit up the team, and recollect Alice's CAG.

With the sounds of horns blaring to warn others to clear the runways, Alice's dropship took off into the air. They sped ahead and as the captain gave them orders

Alice sat on a bench, her kill team amongst her, and she focused her mind.

Kill the Archon. Stop the war.

There would be others—new threats to challenge—but that would have to wait.

It was the scarred Archon's brood that had entered into New York, she could sense that much.

End him and fight and move upon the others.

Alice stood up halfway into the flight, unable to sit any longer. She could see jets scream alongside them through the windows as she paced the center of the dropship.

She connected into the kill team's comms. "You've all heard what's happened. You all know he's alone. We kill him and we cut the head off the snake," she practically screamed the words as she spoke. The ship rattled and all of her team sat on their benches, watching her.

"The Archon isn't like anything we've faced."

Their faceless helmets shifted to follow her movements.

"He's more powerful than anything else, but he's insane and he's alone. We can kill him."

She stopped at the front of the cabin and turned to face the team. She pressed the clasp on her helmet and it popped off. She took it in hand.

She wanted them to see her face.

Her eyes.

"What do you say?" she called out.

The soldiers stomped their feet with a loud *thump-thump-thump.*

"I say we kill the fucker!"

"Jam his head up his ass."

"Berlin Bitch, that's what I fucking say."

"Red Bitch of Berlin!"

"Red Bitch. Red Bitch."

The soldiers chanted and stomped their feet. Alice sat her helmet on her head, it sank down and connected.

The pilot came over the comms.

"Location inbound, locate and enter cages. Prepare for deployment."

Alice moved to her seat and thumped a large wall button.

There were three beeps and flashes from a red light inside her cage, and then the *chunk-chunk-chunk* of metal chains moving as a shoulder brace came down over her and locked her CAG into the seat. There was a loud vibration as the cage doors closed in around her.

The other soldiers snatched up their weapons and moved toward their seats.

And just outside the window, Alice saw a flash of light as a jet exploded.

Her eyes went wide.

He's here.

She hadn't even felt him.

Their own ship rattled suddenly and a loud emergency siren went off.

A grinding sound of twisting metal came from the back of the ship as a hole was torn into the back.

Alice saw the pale, clawed hands of the Archon digging through the metal and entering in.

"Hull breach, hull breach!" the pilot screamed into the comms before panicking and switching to Russian. He continually rattled out words in Alice's ears as she watched.

The ship started to thrash as the Archon sank his claws into the metal of the wall, and used it to claw forward as air pulled through the breach.

One of the Soviets hadn't taken his seat. With one hand holding his cage for balance, he got his rifle out in front of him with the other hand and fired.

The rifle wasn't meant to be fired with a single hand, and it bucked around. There were sparks and flashes as some of the bullets missed and hit the wall, but others found their mark and pounded into the Archon's flesh, making tiny black holes.

Alice struggled to move, but the cage had already locked her in place and she couldn't get out. She reached out with her mind against the Archon, but felt a wall unlike any she'd ever encountered.

The Archon darted forward and grabbed the man firing at him. He hurled him back and the man screamed as he went through the hole in the ship.

Several of the other soldiers had already locked in and they shouted curses at the Archon, and fought just like Alice to get out of the cage.

But the cages were strong, and they were all locked in place.

The Archon turned to one man, already firmly in his cage. The Archon grabbed the door, and pried it open with ease. The soldier, pinned down with the shoulder press, swung a punch, but the Archon batted the man's helmet, and the sound of his head ripping off was loud enough for Alice to hear over all else.

"You motherfucker!" she shouted because she could do anything else. She felt a bead of blood roll down her lip as her mind scratched bloody at the Archon's wall. "I'll kill you!"

The Archon spared her one glance and went to the next man locked in place.

Novikov, the team's captain, had yet to lock in. He turned away from the Archon and moved closer to the pilot. He went to the emergency casing and grabbed a handle and cranked it down—the manual override to drop the cages.

"Kill him, Winters!" Novikov screamed into the comms.

The red light in her cage flashed again. Three flashes that seemed to come much slower than she'd ever seen them before.

After the third flash the ground beneath her gave way and the cage went loose on its rail. She watched as the Archon pried open another man's cage and reared his hand back to kill, but she slid into the air and lost sight.

Several cages dropped around her, and she saw the Archon, caught by surprise, fall out with the man he was trying to kill.

The man's cage was bent and half destroyed so it spun out of control and turned top over bottom over and over.

The Archon fanned his wings out and caught in the air like a parachute as Alice hurled toward the ground. She craned her head up to see the Archon fly at her dropship.

It blew up seconds later, and then she saw his wings flash as he moved toward a second dropship and cut right through it with a fiery explosion.

A jet screamed in the distance and fired a missile. It blazed toward the Archon and impacted him with a blast.

The hive mind echoed with a scream of pain so loud it made her throw her head back.

She looked up again and had to twist her head back and forth to see where the Archon was. Still alive, she caught sight of his wings fan open again and he sped toward the passing jet.

What happened, or what he did, she didn't know, but the jet blew up.

She passed through a cloud and she lost sight of him.

Another dropship went whizzing past her. Dark smoke trailed from it as it hurdled toward the ground.

Around her, other drop cages were speeding through the air, but she was too disoriented to count how many.

The spinning drop cage went whirling through the air and bashed into another before it went sailing off.

The ground came up fast and Alice's cage slammed into the dirt. The shocks absorbed the hit, and her door opened and the shoulder press came off immediately.

The hit cage landed down on its side against a rock and bent in half. The door opened and a dead man in shattered armor rolled out.

With a rifle in hand, Alice glanced into the air.

"Where the fuck is he?" she screamed into her comms as others of her team came out of their cages.

"There, there!" One soldier pointed into the sky and aimed his rifle. Others did the same and their rifles rattled as they fired into the sky.

Alice looked up to see the long wings of the Archon descending upon them.

The soldiers kept firing, but hadn't they seen the missile? Didn't they know about the nuke?

She only knew of one way to kill a god.

Alice fell to her knees and she took a breath, though it might no longer be necessary.

She was human.

And she killed monsters.

———

THIS WORLD WAS REAL.

And it wasn't.

In it sat a king.

A god to all that would become.

The god's hand was bloody.

It was not man's blood.

It was his brother's.

Three kings. Three crowns. Three to rule the world.

Alice saw this truth, he shared it with her as their minds touched.

She knew the rules now.

But why should there be three kings when one would suffice?

He's not my king. He's not my god.

She told herself that as she took a step deeper into the darkness of the void.

He was there before her. A crown of horns growing upon his head.

He sat upon a throne, not because his kind desired such things, but because hers did.

He was more than his brothers.

He knew the beauty of this world.

And he also knew its hate.

Alice hated him.

And with that hate, she drew a knife.

And she thrust it at him.

But it did not kill him, and he did not bleed.

For he was a god.

And she was not.

The Archon stepped down from his throne, and the world shook for that was his will that all should tremble.

Alice stood tall against him and as he approached she drew another knife, formed from the world itself.

But he took her and placed a hand on her face. Alice struggled and she grabbed his thick wrist. His fingers squeezed down against her skull, and small wounds opened and wept.

Blood ran down her face as his fingers dug in.

And little by little.

All that was Alice—all that was human. . .

Began to die.

THE ARCHON STOOD within the real world, surrounded by the bodies of dead men.

A wounded plane careened into the ground some distance behind him, but it didn't so much as draw his attention.

Alice Winters knelt upon the ground before him.

And his focus was on her.

He glared down at her as her body shook. Shaking on her knees, she grabbed her sidearm from her hip and with a shaky hand, pointed it at him.

She blasted two rounds that smacked into his midsection. The bullets hit him and fell off.

What was she trying to do when all else failed?

He grabbed her by the chin and sank his fingers into her helmet.

The metal groaned and cracked as he pulled it free.

Wet strands of blonde hair stuck to her face, and her eyes were wide and panicked as she made uncomfortable breathing noises like a half-strangled animal.

Though her body shuddered, her other hand drew out a knife and held it up.

The Archon snatched her at the wrist. He looked at the hand and then at her.

Something was strange.

He squeezed hard enough to crush the arm and her knife dropped.

Alice Winters ground her teeth and threw her head back gasping in pain. Wires and machinery crackled and clicked beneath the wound.

Curious.

Why would it hurt to destroy such a thing? Had they done work to her to confuse the pain?

He reached down and put his hand on her face. She hissed breath as he started to squeeze.

He'd killed his brother's Janissary for such weakness.

Her skull crunched as his fingers dug in.

Blood poured from her nose and her mouth sagged as her eyes rolled up into her head.

Perhaps he'd pierced her brain and made her a useless thing?

Perhaps not.

It would be an easy thing to finish her.

An easy thing to see her die.

But no.

He wanted the woman.

For she was beautiful.

And she would serve.

26

ERKIN KAHN HAD BEEN FITTED for CAG, but he'd never worn such things before.

It was not a simple tool to master.

His handlers became upset and screamed amongst each other when he stumbled or hit the wrong commands on his gauntlet.

It was clear he didn't have the time to master the weapon system.

They settled on a lightened version that included little more than a chest piece and helmet.

The People's Republic of China had a growing enemy, and time was of the essence.

Accompanied with a team of fully equipped Chinese Red Army commandos, Erkin entered into battle against a small force.

He remembered it was raining so heavily that day he could barely see in front of him, like God had fallen ill of his creation and decided to drown it.

The monsoon season was upon them.

It was strange though, he didn't remember much else.

Only flashes.

A horrible multi-legged thing came from the rain, but if that was before or after Erkin had killed everything else, he couldn't now remember.

Tentacles lashed about it, each a crawling snake hungry for prey.

The soldiers had fired upon it, but Erkin had only lifted a hand.

And just as he built the house inside his mind, here he built a box for the creature and he placed it inside.

Then he crushed it.

It fell over dead and the Chinese soldiers confirmed the kill.

His head soaked with rain, they loaded him back up on a truck and hurried him to a new encounter.

Erkin was tested three more times that day, and each time he did the same.

He built walls around the beast, walls that held it still.

And he brought them down.

Within his mind's eye he could feel the monsters' hearts crushing as if it were happening in his own hand.

He could practically feel the blood running between his fingers.

Wu had been pleased and smiled upon Erkin as he made promises of a future to come should China's enemies be destroyed.

Then Wu gave a command.

"Send him to Beijing."

Erkin stormed the city alongside the Chinese Red Army troops.

Inside his chest armor and helmet CAG, he heard the troops calling out orders as the tanks rolled forward and the men stormed past.

Erkin reached his hands out and built a powerful wall within his mind.

And he pulled it down.

Waves of creatures died before him, and those few that made it through were cut down by rifle fire.

It was a rare thing for the monsoon season to be so far north as Beijing, but it was there again today.

But Erkin did not so much think that God desired to wash his creation away.

Perhaps God wept upon the world.

As powerful as Erkin's walls were, the enemy was more so.

The Jade Archon.

That was the enemy's name. How Erkin knew it, he didn't know, but he was certain that's what the creature's name was.

The Jade Archon.

Rain fell and mixed with the blood on the ground, and it swirled past Erkin's feet as he moved through the streets.

Explosions and screams rattled around him, but he stayed focused, and within his mind, he built war and death.

The lines of the enemy were strong, and they broke through the Chinese Red Army. A tank to Erkin's side was overrun and creatures pulled open the hatch and dragged screaming men loose.

Erkin watched for but a moment before turning away.

A squad of soldiers was overrun and torn apart. Their blood spattered up against Erkin's helmet.

Erkin rubbed the lens so he could see more clearly.

As Erkin walked amongst the creatures, they swam by him.

The soldier's lines broke and some made a valiant effort to cut close and retrieve Erkin, but they too were overwhelmed and died.

But not Erkin.

He walked amongst them and was not given any concern.

He moved through the rain, his arms beginning to shiver from the cold, and made his way to the city center.

He made a call within the darkness of his mind.

Come.

It was not a command, but a request, for one does not make commands of gods.

Erkin continued toward the center, and he felt the presence of the Jade Archon come to greet him.

With the rain battering them, the cronux flowed out until there were none between Erkin and the Jade Archon, but a circle of cronux surrounded them with mumbles and yips.

The Archon, tall and powerful, was beautiful to see.

A god given flesh.

A tail swung behind the Archon and unlike the others, the Jade

Archon had a face much like a man, with eyes that followed Erkin.

Erkin could feel the hollows of the Archon's mind, and Erkin could feel his thoughts.

The Archon knew why Erkin was here.

Erkin had not come to kill.

He had come to conquer.

Erkin closed his eyes and built a box.

The Archon rushed at him.

But Erkin squeezed the box.

And if that box were real. . .

And if it were in Erkin's hands. . .

Then blood would run through his fingers.

And the Jade Archon would die.

Erkin opened his eyes and the Archon was dead upon the field.

The cronux screamed and attacked each other in their frenzy for blood.

Erkin moved a hand and two came screaming out from the crowd. They gathered the Archon and dragged their claws across his scalp to open his head.

They bowed away as Erkin came close.

Instinct drove Erkin as he dug his hands in. . .

And ate the brain.

The cronux howled in praise for they had witnessed a powerful moment.

Pink juice ran between Erkin's fingers as he dug out handfuls of the Archon's brain, and shoved it into his mouth. Each bite made the liquid squeeze between his lips and run down his face, but still he ate.

He began to change.

Soon only the sound of Erkin's nails scratching the inside of the Archon's skull, and his loud chewing were all that could be heard. The cronux had quieted, for this was a hallowed event.

The death of one god...

...the birth of another.

LEI ZHAO, chairman of China, sat behind his desk as Wu entered the room.

Zhao had already heard the news, Wu knew that he did, but it was etiquette within Chinese society to allow Wu to deliver it, as it was his victory.

Wu bowed his head and spoke, "Operation Dragonskin has proven fruitful. The Dragon has entered into Beijing and slain the Archon. Beyond our perception, the Dragon has taken control of the forces and scattered them to the barren regions of inner Mongolian."

"Why haven't they been destroyed?"

"The forces are believed to be beyond ten million. Even with control, it will not be an easy thing to destroy them all. But the Dragon thus remains in command and the forces submit beneath you. Reports are that the American Dragon has fallen. Ours proves the superior being, and China the greater force."

Zhao nodded his head. "Your operation and planning have proven quite useful, Mr. Wu. You will be rewarded for your success."

"The death of China's enemies, and the flourishing of our nation will be reward enough."

"Then you will be rewarded as it is my pleasure."

"As it pleases you, I serve and obey."

"But I do have thoughts and concerns about the Dragon. Why he was kept in custody for so long?"

"I looked into his circumstances. His name is Erkin Kahn. He was kept in custody because of a filing error and his paperwork was destroyed."

Zhao nodded. "And I've read about his family and the promises you made him."

"Yes, Chairman Zhao. Our psychologists have been closely studying him and building a psychological profile for your review. They believed those promises would provide the greatest response within the Dragon."

"And what are their predictions for when he finds out they're dead?"

EPILOGUE

SITTING in the darkness of the room, Roles had time to contemplate things.

He'd just lost Alice Winters.

A contact in the Soviet Union confirmed it.

"Winters went down engaging the Archon. Nearly the whole strike team was eliminated."

Upsetting, certainly, but not unexpected.

Roles was not unprepared.

Moller was already on her way back with parasites in hand.

And Roles had moles that secured precious data from the Chinese on *Operation Dragonskin*.

He'd already selected the first round of candidates for the *Ghost Initiative*.

But all that could wait.

For the moment, all he needed to do was sit in the darkness.

And wait.

Some time later he saw the headlights of a car flash through the windows, and moments later the rattle of a door unlocking, and a man clearing his throat.

"Lights," said the man with a voice harsh from long hours of work.

Roles leaned back in the chair as the man entered into the living room.

Ben McAndrews, the chief of staff for John Winters, froze when he saw Roles sitting in his recliner.

Roles aimed his loaded pistol.

"Hello, Ben. Figured it was time for you and I to have a private talk." His tone never rose above his casual speaking voice.

McAndrews's gaze shifted around the room like he expected it was a gag and he was waiting for everyone else to jump out.

No one did.

His eyes settled on Roles.

"The fuck is this? How did you get in my house?"

Roles frowned. "What? The security? Please, you insult me. I've been doing this longer than you've been alive."

"Get the fuck out, Roles, *now*."

Roles lifted his elbow and aimed the gun squarely at McAndrews chest.

"I'm a professional. I could make this shot in my sleep before you had a chance to move. Now come take a seat."

With his open hand he gestured toward a chair across from him. A coffee table sat between them with an open bottle of whiskey and two glasses.

"We're going to have a little drink, and you're going to talk. Then you're going to take what you can fit on your back and disappear. Now don't pretend again like you don't know what this is about."

An itch tugged at McAndrews face. He still wasn't sure what to believe, but he complied. Breathing hard, he took a seat across from Roles.

Roles settled his arm down, but kept the gun pointed. "Tell me about the Chinese." He reached out and grabbed the bottle.

In the moments it took Roles to take his eyes from McAndrews and focus on the glass, McAndrews had stiffened ready to move.

"Try your luck if you like," Roles said without looking up. "But I'm faster than I look."

McAndrews settled.

Roles smirked and poured the drinks. With the barrel of the gun, he pointed down at the glass.

"Money." McAndrews said, the expressions on his face starting to melt. "It's always about money. What else do you think?"

"Yes, it's always about money." Roles nodded. "Must have been a lot."

"It was." McAndrews picked up the glass and took a drink. "And I have a lot of it in hard currency here in the house, and another chunk in untraceable crypto coins."

"If you're making me an offer, you better hold your tongue. You're only going to piss me off."

McAndrews snorted uncomfortably and shook his head. "You're such a fucking asshole, Roles. Yeah, I told them about Alice. Who gives a fuck? If they keep things locked down in their country, all the better for it."

"Not only Alice, you advocated for them in our meetings. You tipped them off about national priorities."

"*And?*" McAndrews curled his lip and took another drink. "If not me, then someone else. Shoot me if you want, but you're not going to make me feel bad about it."

Roles grunted and picked up his glass. He took a drink.

McAndrews shrugged. "Going to tell me how you found out?"

"You're an idiot. That's how I found out. I only gave two people some bullshit about cryo helping clear the mind of Ghosts, and the Chinese attempted it the very next day." Roles flattened his expression. "Sloppy. Amateurish. You're not suited for this kind of work. I'd recommend you give it up in the next life."

"Clearly. If I was, then I'd be the one holding the gun." He took another drink. "You're going to shoot me after all this, aren't you?"

"Fifteen years ago I would have. Now my back would ache too much from dragging your body around. You finish a few drinks with me, tell me everything that happened, then you fade away. But if you skip any details, I'll risk the back ache.

McAndrews fanned his arms out. "What else do you want to know?"

"The Soviets. I want to know why you helped them too."

McAndrews froze in place. One eye twitched.

"Not much of a poker face there."

"I'm better when there isn't a gun involved."

"You're really testing my patience. When the Soviet sleeper cells moved on Washington, the public at large wasn't aware yet that John Winters had been appointed Secretary of State. Moreover, because of his recent movement into the role, his whereabouts were also unknown but to a few. We've combed through damaged computer systems and we found a coded message between an informer and a sleeper agent." Roles shook the gun at McAndrews like it was a finger and he was naughty. "You gave him away. You were complacent in the assassination of American leadership. Why? *Money?*"

"*Roles.*" McAndrews leaned forward and put his elbows on his knees. He had a look on his face like Roles was naive. "It's *always* about money."

Roles nodded and swallowed the rest of his drink. He let out a little breath and tisked his tongue off his teeth.

"You know I have agents in China and the Soviet Union."

"I know." McAndrews said and took another drink.

"You know how I flip them?"

McAndrews grinned. "Money. An American passport?"

Roles shook his head.

"I promise them a chance to hurt the regime. Those people have had families in the gulags. Fathers on the firing lines. Children in the camps. They don't give a damn about money. They risk death and torture because they want to hurt something."

"What does that—"

Roles snapped his elbow up and fired a silenced round into McAndrews's chest.

McAndrews waved back and forth, spilling his drink. With his mouth gasped, he looked down to the smoking hole in his chest.

Roles held the pistol on him in case another round was required and poured another drink.

McAndrews gasped and rolled his head about until he gave one final breath and deflated in his chair.

The second round wasn't needed.

Roles placed his pistol on the table and leaned back into the chair to enjoy his drink. He was going to need it if he had to drag the body around.

He held it up to his face and watched the booze swirl around as he moved the glass. He looked over the edge at the smoking hole in McAndrews.

"It's sad that all it takes for us is money."

He took a drink.

WHAT'S NEXT?

Want to know the latest on the *Reality Bleed* series?

Join our Facebook group to talk *Reality Bleed* and keep up-to-date on everything that's happening.

HELL ON EARTH

REALITY BLEED BOOK 9

ABOUT J.Z. FOSTER

J.Z. Foster is a writer originally from Ohio. He spent several years in South Korea where he met and married his wife.

He received the writing bug from his mother, NYTimes best-selling author, Lori Foster.

Check out his other books and let him know how you like them!

Write him an email at:
JZFoster@JZFoster.com

WINTER GATE PUBLISHING

Want to stay up to date on the latest from Winter Gate Publishing?
Follow us on Facebook at Facebook.com/WinterGatePublishing to
know more!

Winter Gate Publishing. Reality Bleed: Earth Siege